Christmas Comes to Little Hickman Creek

Christmas
Comes to
Little Hickman Creek

Sharlene MacLaren

WHITAKER
HOUSE

CHRISTMAS COMES TO LITTLE HICKMAN CREEK
A Novella

Sharlene MacLaren
www.sharlenemaclaren.com
sharlenemaclaren@yahoo.com

ISBN: 978-1-62911-180-3
eBook ISBN: 978-1-62911-181-0
Printed in the United States of America
© 2014 by Sharlene MacLaren

Whitaker House
1030 Hunt Valley Circle
New Kensington, PA 15068
www.whitakerhouse.com

Library of Congress Cataloging-in-Publication Data

MacLaren, Sharlene, 1948– author.
 Christmas Comes to Little Hickman Creek / Sharlene MacLaren.
   pages cm. — (Little Hickman Creek Series ; Fourth)
 Summary: "In the very season when the wounds of her heart are most raw, a hurting young
widow named Sadie Bennett learns to love again"—Provided by publisher.
 ISBN 978-1-62911-180-3 (alk. paper)
 1. Widows—Fiction. 2. Kentucky—Fiction. 3. Christian fiction. 4. Love stories. I. Title.
PS3613.A27356C48 2014
813'.6—dc23
                    2014019358

1 2 3 4 5 6 7 8 9 10 11   **ᴧ**   22 21 20 19 18 17 16 15 14

Dedication

For Madelyn Sophia...Grandma's little doll.
How I love you, precious miracle girl—all the way from here
to the moon and back, a thousand times over.

Chapter One

December 1898 · Little Hickman, Kentucky

The town bustled with activity on this chilly, early morning in the first week of December as twenty-six-year-old Sadie Bennett made her way to work at Grace's Tearoom. She hurriedly crossed Main Street, lifting her skirts as she went to keep them from dragging in the filthy mud and horse dung. Actually, her place of employment, owned by the lovely, middle-aged Grace Giles, amounted to much more than a tearoom—it offered hearty breakfasts and overgenerous lunches—but the former Chicagoan had said she wanted to bring a bit of culture to the otherwise raggedy, backwoods town of Little Hickman, Kentucky. Sadie had no idea if the "tearoom" label helped. She tended to think not.

"Morning there, Miss Bennett. Bitter mornin', ain't it?"

She stepped up onto the planked sidewalk and turned to see Tom Flanders, owner of a local food store. The first thing she wanted to do was correct him about her name. It was *Mrs.* Bennett, not *Miss.* True, she'd been married a mere total of four weeks before her beloved had met with his premature death at Grady's Sawmill, where a monstrous limb from a tree they'd been splitting had unexpectedly thundered to the earth, crushing him on impact. It had been a dreadful tragedy, but it didn't erase the fact that she'd been Mrs. Bennett before the accident, and she continued to be so today. She supposed there were some who didn't think that one month of wedded bliss qualified her for carrying on the title; in fact, for all she knew, they'd relegated her to the roster of local spinsters. It surprised her that no one had reverted to calling her by her maiden name, Swanson. Granted, few townsfolk knew her well, since she'd moved to Little Hickman just eight months prior to marrying her longtime sweetheart, Thomas Bennett. He'd followed her and her family—her father and her younger brothers and sisters—here from Frankfort after her mother had died. He'd secured a job almost immediately at the sawmill, bought them a little house just outside of town, and set up housekeeping before they married. If only she could turn back time to that fateful morning of almost two years ago and convince Tom not to go to work that day. So far, however, she hadn't met a single soul who could tinker with Father Time.

"Morning, Mr. Flanders," Sadie finally responded, forcing a bright tone into her voice. "Yes, it's frightfully cold this morning." She pulled her woolen cape a little closer to her neck.

"Hope to high heaven the sun comes out to melt this frost," Mr. Flanders said. "Next thing you know, we'll be gettin' snow, and it wouldn't surprise me, neither, cold as it's been lately."

"Oh, let's hope it doesn't come to that." Sadie wished she could skip right past December—the month when Tom had died—not to mention Christmas. Seeing shopkeepers already starting to bedeck their display windows with holiday cheer certainly did not help matters. Gracious, Christmas was still some twenty days in the offing. Must they rush the holiday to such extremes? Why, in her family, tradition dictated that the Christmas tree not go up till one week prior to the holiday; but just yesterday, she'd noticed the Barrington boy hauling home a good-sized fir tree, chopped off at the base, on the back of his wagon. No doubt it had already been erected in the Barringtons' living room.

Mr. Flanders tipped the brim of his tattered hat at her and made a right turn, while she turned left, her speedy steps clicking in four-four time, the exact rhythm of "God Rest Ye Merry, Gentlemen." Odd, since merry was just about as far as possible from the way she'd been feeling recently. Still, a few of the lyrics thrummed through her head. *Let nothing you dismay...to save poor souls from Satan's power...oh, tidings of comfort and joy, comfort and joy...oh, tidings of comfort and joy....*

She shook her head to shut out the words as she hurried on. Comfort and joy? Hardly.

Grace's Tearoom was already humming with patrons when she opened the door, the little bell above it giving a welcoming tinkle. The tearoom's hours were 7:00 a.m. to 2:00 p.m. every day except Sunday, but Grace was happy to unlock the door early for the regulars who arrived ahead of schedule. A few heads turned at Sadie's entrance, and several people nodded to acknowledge her, while others were too distracted with table talk to even notice her. As usual, Grace gave a friendly wave and a warm smile from behind the counter. Did the woman ever experience a bad day? Sadie had never seen her in a foul mood.

Smells of fried potatoes, eggs, and bacon accosted her, and her stomach reacted with an immediate growl. She closed the door behind her and wended her way past the neatly set tables, unbuttoning her cape as she moved to the back of the restaurant, where several hooks on the walls invited employees and patrons alike to hang their wraps. For most of the year, the hooks sat lonely and unused, but not so these days. In fact, of late, there was often nary a stray hook to be found, and some folks predicted that this might well be the year for a white Christmas. Most even seemed to be praying for it, as snow came so seldom to the rolling hillsides of Kentucky. With a sniff, Sadie removed her cloak and woolen hat, draping both over a coat that already occupied one of the hooks. White Christmas, brown Christmas... neither much mattered to her.

After doing a little business at the bank, Reed Harris crossed the rutted street, stepped up to the sidewalk, and trudged onward, watching his breath come out in puffs—a rare sight indeed for early December. He touched the brim of his hat to acknowledge a couple of women passing by, one of whom carried a wriggling youngster who repeatedly yelped, "I want down!" He passed Flanders Food Store and Winthrop's Dry Goods before stepping down and crossing the alley that led to the town bathhouse.

Thankfully, he'd enjoyed a nice hot bath last night in the comfort of his own little abode on Elm Street. No more trips to the bathhouse for him—no, siree. Being a proud new homeowner afforded him the luxury of his own claw-foot bathtub in a small room off the kitchen. The tub was a bit dingy, to be sure, but it was workable. Of course, he'd had to heat and haul gallons upon gallons of water to the tub, but he hadn't minded one bit, considering he had the bonus of an indoor pump and a cookstove. Growing up in Georgetown, he'd been accustomed to pumping water from a well several yards from the back door, so having a pump handle over the kitchen sink, let alone a real cookstove, made him feel rather like a king in his own private palace. Assuming ownership of his grandfather's livery hadn't made him rich, by any means, but it had assured him of a steady enough income with which to eke out a meager living and pay for the little house he'd purchased from Irwin Waggoner, who had married and moved into his wife's residence.

Reed's grandfather, Sam Livingston, had moved to Louisville to be nearer his children and other grandkids—Reed's aunts, uncles, and cousins. A little over a year ago, when Papaw had offered him the business at a price that was more than reasonable, he'd jumped at the offer. Ten years of living and working in Lexington had been about all the city life he could handle, and he'd been beyond ready to go back to small-town living. Little Hickman fit the bill, no matter that he'd known very few of its citizens when he'd moved in. Recently, he'd started feeling right at home here, having made some good friends—Ben Broughton, Rocky Callahan, and the Reverend Jon Atkins, to name a few. If he'd learned one thing in the past several years, it was that big city living would never be his preferred lifestyle.

The new clock at Little Hickman Bank struck its twelfth gong just as Reed pulled open the door of Grace's Tearoom and walked inside. All around, patrons chomped on their lunches of soup, salad, and sandwiches. The first thing he did was survey the place, looking for Sadie Bennett. Upon sight of her, he squelched his joy by clearing his throat, straightening his back, and strolling with feigned nonchalance to the nearest empty table. He had yet to win over the pretty thing—for Pete's sake, he hadn't even kissed her. Yes, they'd gone on two outings together, but when he'd asked her to accompany him on a third, she'd declined, giving no particular reason other than that she didn't feel ready.

He understood that, even respected it. She was a widow, after all, and had her reservations. When Reed was a boy, he'd lost his sister and his best friend to some sort of coughing disease; and then, when Reed was a young man of sixteen, his father had succumbed to a dread ailment, so he knew a thing or two about deep sorrow. The question was, did he know enough? He couldn't even imagine losing a spouse so early on in marriage.

He settled himself at the small round table close to the pot-belly stove. The heat pouring out of the stove helped to thaw him from his walk across town. He removed his hat and set it on the red-checkered tablecloth.

"Hey there, Mr. Harris. How you doin' on locatin' that Christmas tree for the town?"

Reed craned his neck to face the elderly Clarence Sterling, seated at a nearby table with a couple of his cronies. "Well, I didn't know it was my job to actually find the tree, Mr. Sterling," he answered with a chuckle. "I just volunteered to haul it into town on my livery wagon."

The man shrugged his shoulders. "You gotta get out there and find the perfect tree."

"With the help of some local merchants," Reed put in.

"Hey, isn't Miz Grace Giles on the committee?" piped up Truman Atwater, one of the fellows at Clarence's table.

"Grace Giles what?" Grace approached Reed's table, a pad of paper in hand. Shucks, he'd been hoping Sadie would wait on him, although he had no quarrel with Mrs. Giles.

"We're talking about the Christmas tree that the town council voted to put up this year," Reed said. "You're on the selection committee, remember? Just have to find a time that's convenient for all five members to go out looking."

"I volunteered for that, did I? When?" She tucked a graying strand of hair behind a petite ear. Although she was probably in her late forties, the woman possessed a wealth of youthful beauty.

Reed grinned. "Last summer. I was at the meeting, so you'll be hard-pressed to deny it."

She frowned. "Can I send someone in my place?"

Reed laughed. "Shirking your duties, are you? Shame on you."

"Not at all, Mr. Harris; more like taking them quite seriously. Sadie, come here please," she called across the restaurant, her snappy eyes containing a certain twinkle. Reed's gut rolled over. What did this woman have up her sleeve?

Not more than a few seconds flitted by before Sadie Bennett arrived at her boss's side. "Yes?" When Sadie spotted Reed, a faint blush crept up her neck.

"I'm hereby appointing you to take my place on the Christmas tree selection committee."

"The—the Christmas tree selection committee?" Sadie sputtered. "What sort of committee is that?"

"You will accompany this handsome young man"—Grace nodded to Reed—"and a few other local merchants to the hillsides of Little Hickman in search of the perfect Christmas tree."

"The perfect—" Sadie glanced nervously at Reed. "Oh, but...I...."

"Now, now, no arguing with me. I haven't the time for one more committee, but I happen to know you do."

"I do?" Sadie cast her employer a plaintive look.

"Yes, you do. In fact, wait on this kind gentleman for me, would you?" She handed her pad of paper to Sadie, then turned and marched back to the kitchen.

"I don't need—" Sadie began, as if the woman could hear her. Obviously flustered, she gave her head several harried shakes, which caused a number of loose strands of her ink-black hair to fall away from their side combs. Blessed stars above, was she ever pretty!

"Well, that should work out jes' fine, havin' Miz Sadie take Miz Grace's place," said Clarence Sterling.

Reed grinned at the ruffled waitress. Yes, siree, just fine indeed. "I'll have the toasted cheese sandwich and a big bowl of potato soup, if you don't mind."

Saying not a word, she nodded and turned on her heel. With a great deal of satisfaction, Reed watched her stomp back to the kitchen, her long skirts billowing, her heels clicking loudly on the wood floor.

Chapter Two

*S*adie couldn't believe she'd allowed Grace to volunteer her to serve on the Christmas tree selection committee. She had no desire to go in search of a suitable Christmas tree for Little Hickman's town square, which amounted to nothing more than a roped-off section in the middle of Main Street, smack-dab in the center of town between Flanders Food Store and Bordon's Bakery. Why, they'd be lucky if galloping horses didn't plow it over. Drivers and riders did not always take their sweet time when traveling through town, much as Sheriff Murdock tried to enforce the speed limit.

She'd learned that the other four locals who'd volunteered to select the tree were Tom Flanders, Iris Winthrop, Harvey Coleson, and Emma Atkins. She was happy about Emma, proprietress of the boardinghouse in Little Hickman; but the others, particularly Iris Winthrop, could make this a less than thrilling experience. How in the world would everyone come to the same conclusion about a tree? She determined to keep her opinions to herself and let the rest of them—namely, the officious, overbearing Mrs. Winthrop—make the final decision. Would the others be as accommodating?

Then there was the matter of the driver, Mr. Harris. Sadie had accompanied him to the Independence Day Community Picnic and then to an autumn barnyard dance. Both times, she'd enjoyed herself—though almost begrudgingly. It just hadn't felt right taking pleasure in the company of another man—not when the loss of her sweet Tom remained so fresh in her mind. Oh, it wasn't that Reed Harris wasn't as handsome as an 1890 hundred-dollar bill. For heaven's sake, his buckskin hair, broad-shouldered physique, square-set face, and deep emerald eyes had to make him the best catch, physically speaking, in all of Little Hickman. Even so, she couldn't muster the mood for investing her time and energy in him. She trusted the Lord, but, good glory, that didn't make life any less risky or uncertain. What if she grew attached to Mr. Harris, and something terrible happened to him, as well? Even now, while readying herself to walk to Sam's Livery—well, it was *Reed's* Livery now—she shuddered at the thought.

She fastened the strings of her wool bonnet in a bow under her chin, tucked a few stray wisps of hair underneath, and then wrapped a scarf around her neck. It was another day of gray skies and biting wind, and to make matters worse, an entire three inches of snow had fallen overnight—an almost unheard-of event before Christmas. Not only did she not wish to traipse through

snow in search of a Christmas tree, she didn't relish freezing her
nose off in the process. With luck, another committee would be
in place to erect the tree once they brought it into town, and still
another to decorate it—although she'd heard rumors that the
decorating would take place later in the week, a sort of community event, with everyone contributing ornaments. Iris Winthrop
had announced her intention to furnish the star for the top. *Of
course, she would*, Sadie thought. No one enjoyed adulation more
than Mrs. Winthrop. Co-owner and operator of Winthrop's Dry
Goods with her husband, Clyde—quieter and far more pleasant
than his wife—she always made it a point to draw attention to
her accomplishments or to point out the finer aspects of her store
as compared to Johansson's Mercantile.

Although Sadie had nothing against the idea of a town
Christmas tree, she had no real enthusiasm for participating in
any holiday festivities. Rather, she would much prefer working
by day and hibernating by night in her tiny three-room dwell-
ing situated above Bordon's Bakery. Today marked the two-year
anniversary of Tom's death, and if she could have, she would have
curled up in a little ball and slept till Christmas had come and
gone.

Her kitchen clock read ten minutes to three, and since the
consensus had been to gather at the livery at three o'clock on
Saturday, she decided she'd better make her way there. She
removed her woolen coat from its hook by the door, slipped into
it, and buttoned it clear up to her throat. May as well prepare for
the unusually cold weather. Hopefully, the day would not drag
on, and she'd be back in plenty of time to enjoy her supper of beef
stew and bread. Alone.

The other committee members arrived at the livery at three on the dot, with the exception of Iris Winthrop, who'd come fifteen minutes ahead of schedule and then proceeded to complain that the others hadn't done the same. Since Reed had little desire to listen to her grievances, he'd attempted to make light conversation while harnessing his horses to the wagon.

He couldn't quite envision Iris Winthrop sitting comfortably on one of the hay bales, but if she held on tightly to the bars, she should be okay. He didn't worry about Emma Atkins, the reverend's wife. While pretty, she struck him as hale and hearty, particularly since she'd operated Emma's Boardinghouse for years as a single woman with nary a problem, despite the houseful of rough-and-tumble characters who rented rooms from her. He did worry a tad about Sadie Bennett. He didn't want to be liable for anyone bouncing off the wagon, and she struck him as one who had the strength of a fallen leaf. Little Hickman's back roads were nothing if not bumpy and unsafe, and then there was the creek to cross, and one never knew how high the water might be on any given day. Add to that the few inches of slushy snow that had accumulated, and he fretted that the drive might get a little complicated.

When Sadie arrived, she made eye contact with everyone but him. Clearly he made her nervous, and he wished with everything in him that he knew how to settle those fears. It wasn't as if he intended to force himself on her.

"Should we set off?" asked Harvey Coleson, who worked at Zeke's Barbershop. In fact, Reed had just sat in his chair last Saturday.

"Sounds good," said Tom Flanders, rubbing his gloved hands together. "Let's get this over and done. It's too cold to be dallying."

"We may get ourselves situated in the wagon," said Iris Winthrop, lips stretched into a tight line, "but I believe we should discuss some guidelines before departing."

"Guidelines?" Harvey grunted. "Ain't we just out to find us a suitable tree—a tall, full, round one, with a good shape—somethin' we can all admire? Wull, I'll be dipped in lizard gravy if I ain't just described my own wife—tall, round, and well-shaped!"

"Mr. Coleson!" Iris Winthrop exclaimed.

The men all chuckled, and even Emma gave a hearty laugh; but Iris glared, and Sadie pressed her lips together, as if to avoid smiling.

"Oughtn't be too difficult a task if we keep ar eyes open," said Harvey. "Let's climb aboard and talk as we're ridin'."

Iris harrumphed, and when Harvey tried to help her aboard, she slapped his hand away, choosing instead to grasp hold of the vertical bar and step up onto the overturned crate unassisted, huffing and puffing, until she'd settled herself on a hay bale. She made quite a sight, if Reed did say so, with her enormous bustle, heavy coat, and oversized hat. Emma, conversely, thanked Harvey and accepted his hand, as did Sadie Bennett, even though she seemed to take extra care to hold her slender shoulders erect and her back straight.

As they journeyed out of town, the men did most of the talking, with Emma inserting a few comments here and there. Iris and Sadie remained quiet. Reed was pretty sure Iris was still stewing, but he couldn't tell what was going through Sadie's mind. Since she was sitting directly behind him, while he stood behind the buckboard, steering his team, he decided to strike up a conversation with her.

He turned his head around for a quick glimpse. "You enjoy your job at the restaurant?"

A startled expression lit her features, but she quickly recovered and glanced up at him. "Yes, very much. It keeps me busy and brings in enough income to make ends meet."

"That's good," he said with a nod. "And since that little restaurant is always busy, I expect it's also afforded you the opportunity to get to know some of the townsfolk. Little Hickman's a friendly place, don't you think?"

"Very friendly."

"Have you lived in these parts all your life?" he ventured. He realized he'd never inquired about her past on their two previous outings, mostly because he'd been afraid of stirring up sorrow over her late husband.

"No. I grew up in Frankfort. I came here with my father and my younger siblings after my mother passed away a few years ago. We moved to my uncle's vacant farmhouse, and my father has been farming the land for him and enjoying it very much. I helped him with my siblings until he remarried. Then, not long after, I married, as well."

His chest gave a little jolt at the mention of her marriage. Had she intended it to remind him that she remained untouchable?

"And when was that?"

"Pardon?"

"When did you marry?" he risked asking.

"November third—two years ago. My husband died very shortly after that. Actually, the accident happened two years ago today."

A tight gasp of air nearly choked him when it hit his lungs. "Really? Two years today?" He swung his head around to cast her a quick glance.

The others on the wagon ceased conversing.

"Oh, Sadie. How insensitive of me not to have thought about that," said Emma. "I remember that day so vividly, but I didn't realize today was the second anniversary. I'm so sorry."

"As am I," said Reed, unable to think of anything further to say. He stared straight ahead, his chest fairly stinging with emotion.

"That was a downright tragedy," said Harvey.

Iris cleared her throat. "This is quite a day for you, then, searching for a Christmas tree. Do you wish to go back?"

"No, I'm fine. Really. If I'd stayed holed up in my little apartment, I probably would have spent the day sulking. But thank you, all of you, for your concern. Please, I didn't mean to turn an otherwise festive day into one of gloom."

A few seconds of obvious reflection passed over them. "Well, we're glad you came," Tom finally said. "Ain't we glad, folks?"

"Yes!" they all answered in unison.

Quiet conversation resumed, but Reed didn't readily join in. Instead, he reflected a moment on the sawmill accident about which he'd heard only very little a year after the fact, when he'd moved to Little Hickman. There'd been no charges filed against the company, but he'd heard that the judge had ordered the owner of the sawmill, Bill Grady, to enforce stricter standards of safety. Working the mills could be a dangerous profession.

At the first lull, he resumed conversing. "Anybody got special plans for Christmas?" He veered his team of horses to the side of the road to make way for an oncoming buggy, then nodded at the old farmer as he passed. The snow made it difficult to see the road, but tracks from other horses and buggies helped.

"Me an' Irma plan to drive over to Nicholasville to spend the day with her sister," Tom said. "I 'magine we'll be havin' quite a feast. There'll be nieces and nephews in the mix, so it'll get a little rowdy, too."

"It'll be much the opposite for Clyde and me," said Iris. "With no children and no close relatives, we'll likely spend the day by the fire, cracking walnuts and reading the Christmas story."

The normally cranky woman's admission surprised Reed. He wondered if the mention of the sawmill accident had opened a small doorway in her heart and made her a bit more vulnerable.

"And you, Sadie?"

"Oh, I suppose I'll spend the day with my family."

"Of course." Reed nodded. "Nothing like family." With his father gone, his mother and stepfather residing in Chattanooga, and his brother, sister-in-law, and nieces and nephews living clear down in South Carolina, he prepared for another Christmas alone. It didn't bother him. He'd spent other Christmases by himself and had always found plenty to do. He'd probably even keep the livery open for those visitors coming into town who would need to put up their horses for a night or two.

"You live in that little apartment above Bordon's Bakery, don't you?" Iris asked Sadie.

"Yes. My husband had bought us a house, but I sold it after he…died."

"Well, it's nice to live in the center of town," Reed observed. "Just think—you'll be able to see the Christmas tree when you look out your window."

"Yes, won't that be lovely?" said Emma.

"Indeed," Sadie said, her tone lacking enthusiasm.

"Speaking of the Christmas tree, where are we going, Mr. Harris?" Iris asked. "It's getting mighty cold. I surely hope you don't intend to go far."

"Oh, sorry, I should have made that clear. I'm heading down to the Callahan farm. Rocky said he has a nice collection of pine trees growing at the back of his property. Thought we'd check them out. He said if we find one we like, we can help ourselves. You all game for that?"

"Absolutely," said Emma. "Did you bring the tools for cutting it down?"

"We have the tools and the brawn, right, men?" Reed replied. "It's up to you ladies to pick out the perfect tree. Of course, you're welcome to take your turns with the saw, if you wish."

Iris snorted. "No, thank you. I'll leave that to the menfolk."

"I'll take a turn," the ever-cheerful Emma chimed in. "And I bet Sadie will, as well."

"I'm not handy with tools," Sadie said, "but I might give it a try." Without looking back, Reed *heard* a tiny smile in her voice, and he called that progress. It had probably felt good to air the fact that today marked the two-year anniversary of the sawmill accident.

They crossed the creek without incident and made their way to the Callahans'. After trudging up and down several rows, they found what everyone unanimously deemed the perfect tree. Of course, Iris had articulated her opinion of each tree they considered, and whenever anyone had suggested one he thought particularly nice, she found something to dislike about it. In fact, she and Harvey Coleson had become embroiled in a rousing dispute, until Reed had stepped between them and ruled that they wouldn't pick a tree until they reached a consensus—even if it kept them from returning to town till Monday. That had quieted Iris. In the end, they'd chosen a full, tall, perfectly shaped tree in the fir family, with sturdy, well-positioned branches conducive for holding loads of ornaments. The miracle of it was that Harvey Coleson spotted it first, and Iris Winthrop approved. Reed suspected that she was growing cold and simply wanted to head back to town.

With some effort, the men cut down the tree, then dragged it over to the wagon and hefted it up. Emma and Sadie did try their hand with the saw, but their attempts were laughable, and they took the teasing in stride. It warmed Reed's heart to see a genuine smile from Sadie, Emma's good humor helping. The tree took up most of the floor space of the wagon, so folks squeezed together on one side, Mrs. Winthrop grumbling about her discomfort but the others making the best of the situation.

Back in town, a crew of three men—Ben Broughton, Tim Warner, and Truman Atwater—met the group, ready to help erect the tree. They'd already fashioned a large box-shaped stand out of wood and fitted a tubular piece of metal down through the middle to hold the trunk in place. Reed figured they had the tools needed to secure it so that even the strongest wind wouldn't blow it over. He could hope, anyway. With the women watching, the men all unloaded the tree, trimmed off several bottom branches, and then together set the thing in place. Once done, they stepped back in astonished wonder at how straight and tall it stood. After a few minor adjustments, Ben bent down and pressed several pieces of wood between the tube and the trunk to better secure it, and it didn't budge so much as an inch. "It's in there nice and snug-like," he said.

By now, a small crowd of adults and children had gathered to watch the proceedings, and at Ben's pronouncement, they cheered and gave a round of applause. The children jumped up and down with excitement. It would seem that the town Christmas tree had already won the hearts of many, and it wasn't even decorated or lit yet.

Chapter Three

Sadie dried the last plate and set it on top of the tall stack on the shelf above the stove. Then she wiped down the big counter, rinsed out the cloth, and draped it over the edge of the sink. "Done!" she announced.

"That was a lot of dishes," Grace said, approaching the kitchen after cleaning the last table. It was half past three on Tuesday afternoon, an hour and a half after closing time. "We had a big lunch crowd today."

"It's your scrumptious cooking that draws folks."

"I wouldn't say that. Everybody's Christmas shopping, and that'll work up your appetite."

"You're too humble," Sadie said, perusing the kitchen for any stray crumbs. "I doubt Sheriff Murdock went Christmas shopping today."

"Well, he had to eat, I suppose."

"He's been taking all his meals here for the past month, both breakfast and lunch. Have you noticed?"

Grace kept her eyes averted. "Has he now? I can't say I've paid much attention."

Sadie couldn't hold back her smile. "Oh? And I suppose you haven't noticed the way he watches you, either. And strikes up conversations with you whenever possible."

"Pfff." Grace flicked her wrist. "He's just being friendly."

"Um-hmm. He's interested in you, Grace Giles."

"He's an old bachelor."

"He's not so old. I'd guess him to be in his late forties, if that, and he's nice-looking, if you ask me. I've noticed him coming to church lately, too."

Grace chewed on her lower lip. "Yes, I guess he has, now that you mention it."

Sadie giggled. "You like him!"

"Oh, poo."

"You do! He's a good man, Grace."

Grace whisked past her, folded her cleaning rag, and set it on the counter, then started untying her apron. With her back to Sadie, she said, "And I suppose you're going to deny you have feelings for Reed Harris." She hung her apron on its usual hook next to Sadie's yellow one.

Sadie sucked in a quiet breath and let it out. "I can't afford myself the luxury of falling for another man."

Grace whirled around, her pretty mouth set in a frown. "Why would you say a thing like that? He's a fine Christian man, and I happen to know he escorted you on a couple of outings. Didn't you enjoy yourself?"

Sadie glanced out the front window. Several citizens hurried past, packages in hand, coat collars turned up, and faces pointed down to ward off the wind that whistled around the building. At least the snow had melted after only a day or so. "I suppose I did, but…well…Tom was my life, Grace. It's just not right going out with another man."

Grace came close and put her hand on Sadie's arm. "Of course he was your life, honey, but he's been gone for two years. When my husband died, back in eighty-six, I, too, felt lost for a while. That's only natural. Still, Tom wouldn't want you pining away, and neither does the Lord. Each day has something bright and wonderful to offer."

"I suppose." Sadie left the kitchen and made her way to the back of the restaurant to retrieve her winter wrap. She knew Grace watched with sympathetic eyes. She seized her wool cape from its hook and slipped into it, then secured her matching scarf. Meeting Grace's eyes again, she gave a loud sigh and let her shoulders slump. "Truth be told, I don't like Christmas one bit. Is that awful to say?"

Grace gave a little chuckle. "Not awful, no, especially since I understand why you feel that way. You lost your husband so close to the holiday, it's bound to stir up memories. I suppose you're a little put out with me for making you take my place on that Christmas tree committee."

"No I'm not, silly. It turned out not to be so bad."

"Good." She smiled. "Did Mr. Harris have much to say to you? Perhaps by way of an invitation to another social engagement?"

"Well, he did walk me back to my apartment after the tree had been delivered and set up. When we arrived at the bakery, he asked if I'd like to keep walking and talking, but it was just too cold, so I turned him down."

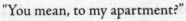

"Did you consider inviting him upstairs for a cup of hot chocolate?"

"You mean, to my apartment?"

"No, to the frozen creek. Of course, to your apartment."

"That wouldn't be appropriate."

"Why ever not?"

"I barely know him."

"And how do you expect to get to know him if you don't give him a chance?"

"Who said I wanted to?"

Grace tilted her head to the side and narrowed her eyes to slits. "You want to. You're just scared."

Choosing not to dignify her comments with a response, Sadie tied her scarf snug around her neck. It was just a short walk across the street and down a few buildings to her peaceful little abode, but she already had a chill running through her. She allowed herself a brief reminiscence of when Reed had accompanied her back to the bakery and asked if she wanted to keep walking. "What are you going to do with the rest of your day?" he'd asked, wearing a crooked grin. "Sit up there and sulk?"

"No, I'm going to enjoy some quiet time—and eat my supper of stew," she'd answered in haste.

"Mmm. Stew sounds good about now. Did you make enough for two?"

She'd looked at her winter shoes and said nothing. She knew a hint when she heard one.

"I'm sorry," Reed had said. "That was outright bold of me, wasn't it? Can you pretend I didn't just invite myself for supper?"

She'd managed a small grin. "I'll try."

He'd dared to reach up and place a curled index finger beneath her chin, gently lifting, so that she'd been forced to look into his eyes. "Listen, about today...I'm glad you came. It was brave of you, you know, with its being the two-year mark of your husband's passing."

His hot breath on her cold cheeks had only made her shivers worse. She'd taken a step back, so he'd dropped his hand to his side, but his gaze on her had never wavered. She hadn't stood so close to a man that handsome since Tom, even though the two couldn't have looked more different. Tom had been tall and lanky but smaller-boned, while Reed Harris fairly towered over her.

"Tom was wonderful," she'd finally said, "and...there will never be another like him." She'd wanted to make that good and clear.

His breath had warmed the air so that it formed puffy clouds that quickly dissipated. "I know a thing or two about grief, Sadie." This he'd said in a husky whisper.

That had spiked her interest. "How so?"

"Well, first, my sister died when I was a young teen. It was some sort of fever, and it was running rampant. A close school pal of mine died about a week after she did of the same ailment. Then, when I was sixteen, my pa died. Consumption was what they called it. It broke my mother up, and I had to be the strong one. Made me grow up pretty darned fast."

Her heart had ached for him, which had surprised her. She wasn't accustomed to reacting to any pain besides her own. "I'm sorry. And your mother...where is she now?"

"She remarried and moved down to Chattanooga. She found a good guy. I have an older brother, too. He lives in South Carolina with his wife and kids. I've come to depend a lot on the Lord when hard times hit, Sadie. How 'bout yourself?"

She'd hesitated. "I have a strong faith, but...well, it's probably nothing like yours."

A low chuckle had formed deep in his throat. "We all have room to grow. Come on, let's go for a walk," he'd urged her. "It'll be good for you. You can tell me about Tom."

She hadn't liked that he presumed to know what was good for her. And other than her father, she'd never discussed her husband with another man, much less someone who had the power to make her heart pound at a strangely fast rate.

"Thank you, but…no, thank you," she'd finally replied.

She recalled how he'd given an audible sigh and shoved his hands in his pockets, then stared down at her with those emerald eyes, as if he knew some unnamed secret. "I'll see you another time, then. How's that?"

She'd nodded. "Good evening, Mr. Harris."

"Call me Reed."

"All right." She'd granted him a tiny smile before ducking inside. That had been all, but she'd known without looking back that he'd watched her through the pane until she'd disappeared from view.

"You are, aren't you?" Grace persisted, starling her back to the present. "Admit it."

Her mind scrambled to recall what they'd been discussing. "I'm what?"

"Scared of falling in love with Reed Harris."

"Oh, for goodness' sake, Grace Giles. You're talking foolishness." She blew out a weighty breath and marched to the door. When she opened it, a blast of cold air tangled around her ankles.

"See you tomorrow, Sadie."

She turned to smile and wave good-bye.

Later that evening, Sadie heard a bit of a hubbub outside her apartment, so she went to the window and pulled aside the heavy curtain. Down below, a large crowd had gathered around the Christmas tree to decorate it. Traffic had literally stopped; anyone who wanted to drive through town would have to travel one block north or south to bypass the commotion. She watched with mild interest. At church on Sunday, Reverend Atkins had encouraged folks to attend the holiday festivities so as to help spread Christmas cheer and share the love of Christ with their fellow citizens. Afterward, some of the church ladies would be serving donated refreshments in the churchyard, and he wanted as many parishioners to come as could make it. A tiny snippet of guilt trickled through Sadie for having no interest in spreading Christmas cheer. With her sewing and knitting abilities, she easily could have created a couple of colorful ornaments for the tree, even though her heart wouldn't have been in it.

A loud disturbance downstairs, followed by a thunder of footsteps and riotous laughter, filled the hallway outside her apartment. Soon after, there came a pounding at her door. What on earth? She scurried to the door and flung it wide. There stood her four siblings, ranging in size from a few feet tall to five feet six inches, her fifteen-year-old brother being the oldest and tallest of the bunch, her younger brother and three younger sisters descending in height like stair steps, each one bearing the same dark hair as Sadie's. She'd been an only child for some years before her mother had finally had a second, third, fourth, and then fifth child, several miscarriages having followed Sadie's birth. Among other features, her mother's Italian roots had produced a string of tan-skinned brunettes.

"Hey, sis," said Daniel, a crooked grin on his handsome face. Immediately, Elizabeth, the six-year-old, charged at her and wrapped her arms around her middle. Then Jacob Michael, eight, and Nora, twelve, took turns giving her a quick hug. "Thought we'd drag you down to the celebration goin' on outside," said Daniel. "Pa an' Miranda are down on the street waiting for you."

"Oh, I didn't plan—"

"We don't care what you planned, sister dear." Daniel strode past her and removed her cape from its hook. "Here you go," he said, handing it over. He found her scarf and hat on another hook. "You'll need these, as well. There's a nip in the air."

She looked from one sibling to the next and twisted her mouth into a slight frown that soon evolved into a grin. "You stinkers. How did you get in without a key?"

Daniel laughed. "Simple. Mr. Bordon is downstairs working in the kitchen. He recognized us and let us in. Now, come on, or you'll miss all the fun."

With only a bit of reluctance, she donned her winter garments. How could she possibly say no to all these dark-eyed darlings?

Chapter Four

Mrs. Winthrop has graciously donated a beautiful star for the top of the tree," Reverend Atkins was announcing through a megaphone as he stood on a small makeshift platform next to the Christmas tree. "Our very own Clyde Winthrop did the honors of securing it at the top. Don't you think he did a fine job?"

As folks gave a loud cheer and a hearty round of applause, Reed approached the crowd and found a place to stand on the periphery of the circle. Thanks to his height, he had a good vantage point—so good, in fact, that it didn't take long for his gaze to land on Sadie Bennett. It made him happy to see she'd braved the throng, though her presence did surprise him somewhat. He wondered what had prompted her to come, but then he saw her bend to speak with a little wisp of a girl and then pull playfully on her braid. One of her siblings, perhaps? She turned and spoke to several other people, folks he recognized from church but had never formally met. They had to be her family members, for he'd spotted her seated in the pew with them on more than one occasion. He hadn't spoken to her since Saturday, wanting to give her some breathing room, lest he come across as some kind of obnoxious, hovering brute. For that reason, he'd also stayed away from Grace's Tearoom.

He watched her now as she interacted with her family. Jon Atkins continued speaking through the large cone-shaped mouthpiece, his deep clarion voice carrying to the masses. He was giving instructions to those who wanted to help decorate the tree, asking that everything be done in an orderly manner, with small children first, assisted by their parents, followed by the older youngsters. "Let's make this a fun family event," he said. "When we've completed the decorating, we'll stand around the tree and sing a few Christmas carols, led by Carl Hardy. After that, I hope y'all will join us at Little Hickman Community Church for cookies and hot chocolate served by some of the ladies of our congregation."

He made a few more announcements before inviting folks to the Sunday services and, of course, to the annual children's program on Christmas Eve.

A powerful slap on the shoulder gave Reed a sudden jolt. "Hey there, my friend. How are you?"

Turning, he broke into a grin at the sight of Rocky Callahan. "Hey, yourself. I'm fine. And you?"

"Never better."

Reed peeked around Rocky's bulky frame. "You here by yourself?"

"Naw, Sarah and the kids are here. They left me in the dust, so I have to work my way through the crowd to reach 'em. Kids're so excited to put their ornaments on the tree. Good idea Jon had for the church to sponsor the event. Sure drew a big crowd."

Reed nodded. "I think the whole town came out."

Rocky looked out over the throng. "Wouldn't surprise me. Well, I best catch up with my family. That's what I get for stopping to talk to folks. You comin' over to the church later?"

"Not sure yet. Probably."

"Good. I'll look for you."

They shook hands before Rocky disappeared into the crowd. Reed watched him go, then debated whether to head for home or hang around to watch some of the decorating. The evening air wasn't particularly mild. In fact, he had to keep shifting from one foot to the other to hold the chill at bay. Not only that, but he'd spent the day mucking stalls, rubbing down horses, and hauling feed—he figured he smelled like a barn, or worse.

He glanced out over the crowd for one more glimpse of Sadie but failed to spot her. Somewhat disappointed, he made the decision to start moving in the direction of home. Perhaps he would clean up a bit, grab a bite to eat, and then venture back to the church to visit with a few of the townsfolk. The night was still young.

He skirted around the edge of the gathering, stepped up to the sidewalk, and passed Winthrop's Dry Goods, noting the big "Closed" sign on the door. Had it not been for the tree decorating ceremony, Little Hickman would've been as still as figures in a tintype, since merchants locked their doors at 5:30 every evening. Even the old saloon that used to operate into the wee hours of the night had shut down a couple of years ago. Truth told, nothing much happened in the town past dusk—and Reed liked it that way.

A jab in his side and a pair of dark eyes staring up at him stopped him in his tracks. "Hey, mister, I think I'm lost," the lad said. For being lost, he didn't look all that worried.

Reed bent at the waist. "What's your name?"

"Jacob Michael Swanson."

"Jacob Michael Swanson," he repeated, trying to place where he'd seen the boy before. Hadn't he been sitting in the same church pew as Sadie last Sunday? "Is Sadie Bennett your sister, by chance?"

The boy tipped his head to the side. "How'd you know that?"

"I've seen you sitting next to her in church." He extended his hand. "I'm Reed Harris. I run the local livery." They shook hands like old friends. "Stick with me, okay? We'll find your family."

"Let's split up. You younger ones stick with Sadie," Sadie's father was saying, his voice edged with mild concern. "Miranda and I will circle that way around, and, Daniel, you go that direction. Sadie, how 'bout you and the two girls head into the center of the hubbub? He can't have gone too far."

Of all Sadie's siblings, Jacob Michael was the most adventurous. Nothing seemed to faze him—not even getting lost in a large crowd. She would scold him plenty for wandering off once she found him, though it wasn't her job to parent him. With Elizabeth in her arms and Nora at her side, she pressed through the throng.

"I want to hang some ornaments," Elizabeth whined.

"You will, honey, just as soon as we find Jacob Michael," Sadie assured her.

"Why'd he have to go off?"

"I don't know. That's Jacob Michael for you. Now, don't fuss."

Folks had already started gathering around the tree, small children first, as the reverend had instructed, their parents right behind them. Sadie didn't quite understand their wild enthusiasm for hanging a few ornaments on the big tree, but then, it took great effort for her to work up any enthusiasm for Christmas.

They bumped against folks as they meandered through the crowd, Nora looking one direction and Sadie another. "I think I see him," Nora finally announced.

"Really? Where?"

"Over there." Nora pointed toward the Christmas tree.

Sadie searched the area with her eyes. "I don't see him."

"He's standing up there with that—that man."

"Up there?" Sadie glanced at the podium where the reverend had stood to make his announcements. There was her little brother—with Reed Harris. Reed scanned the crowd intently, while Jacob Michael wore a happy expression of utter abandon, no doubt enjoying his aerial view of the crowd.

"That stinker," Sadie muttered. "Come on, Nora."

They wended their way back through the masses, little Elizabeth growing heavy in her arms.

"Who's he with?" Nora asked.

"The livery owner."

"I've seen him at church. All the girls think he's handsomer than a prince."

"What?" Sadie paused only slightly to cast Nora a scolding glare. "You're not supposed to be looking at boys, much less men!"

"Why not?" She shrugged. "I'm almost grown."

"I don't want to hear it," Sadie grumbled. It was hard to envision her sister growing into a regular young lady—and a pretty one, at that.

They reached the podium, and before even greeting Reed, Sadie glared at Jacob Michael, whose eyes connected with hers almost immediately. "What are you doing wandering off, young man? You scared your pa something fierce."

Evading her question, he hooked his thumb at Reed. "This here's Mr. Harris. He owns the livery. He rescued me."

Sadie exchanged glances with Reed. "Yes, we've met. Hello again, Mr. Harris. You rescued him?"

"Hi, Sadie. I figured this young fellow belonged with you. I've seen you sitting together in church." He set his hand on Jacob Michael's capped head. "I was heading back to my place when he and I bumped into each other. He admitted he'd sort of lost his way, so I offered to help him locate his family. I knew you were somewhere about, as I'd spotted you earlier." Without giving her a chance to respond, he let his eyes roam over Elizabeth and then Nora. "Beauty tends to run in your family, I see."

"Oh, gracious, I don't know about that." Sadie set Elizabeth down, and the girl played shy, hiding behind Sadie's cape. "People do tend to say we all resemble our mother. This is Elizabeth. Elizabeth, say hello," she urged, but the child kept her face hidden. "And this is my sister Nora."

"Hello there, Nora." Reed stuck out his hand, and Sadie had to nudge her sister in the side to remind her of her manners. The girl's dark eyes bulged, as if she'd just come face-to-face with President McKinley, but then she regained composure and placed her hand in Reed's. Sadie could have sworn she heard a little gush of air rush out of her.

"Thank you for rescuing my brother," Nora squeaked out. Reed removed his hand before Nora appeared ready to let it go. "Although you needn't have. He can be a bit of a pain."

"Nora," Sadie scolded.

"Well, it's true."

"Y'r a bigger pain," said Jacob Michael. "You're always standin' in front of the mirror combin' y'r hair like you was a queen or somethin'."

"Am not!" Had dusk not settled in already, Sadie was sure Nora's face would've shown crimson. As it was, Little Hickman's flaming streetlights cast but a dim glow on her sheepish expression.

"That's enough, you two," Sadie put in.

Reed gave a low chuckle.

"Ah, there you are."

Sadie turned at the sound of her father's voice.

"Where did you go off to, young man?" he asked his youngest son.

"Nowhere. I was just watchin' people, an' the next thing I knowed, you was gone."

Her father made his best attempt at a stern face. "Uh, we did not budge, Son. I believe what you did was move deeper into the crowd without my permission. Now then, how did you wind up on this podium?"

Jacob Michael pointed his finger at Reed. "This man found me. We climbed up here to get a better look around. It was fun. Oh, this is Mr. Harris."

Sadie's father smiled at Reed. "Mr. Harris...ah, yes, you're the one who bought the livery from Sam Livingston. Your grandfather, correct?"

"Yes, sir. Name's Reed. I've seen you and your family in church, but I don't believe we've formally met."

They shook hands. "Yes, yes, of course. Paul Swanson. Nice to finally make your acquaintance."

Miranda soon approached, Daniel at her side, and the introductions continued, followed by a bit more conversation. In time, Elizabeth grew restless and tugged on Sadie's skirts. "Can we go hang ar' ornaments now?"

"Yeah, can we?" said Jacob Michael.

"Well"—Reed stepped back—"you have a nice evening, now." He stole a small glance at Sadie before turning, and an odd frisson raced down her spine.

"Well, just a minute there, Reed—why don't you join us?" her father put in. "We plan to take part in the decorating and caroling and then head over to the church for refreshments."

"Yes, come," said Daniel and Jacob Michael in unison.

Sadie said nothing; she was focused on tamping down the awful churning in her stomach.

"I...well...I had planned to go home and change," Reed stammered.

"Naw, no need," her father said. "Look at me—I'm still in my farm clothes, as is half of Little Hickman."

"Please do join us," said Miranda in her ever-congenial manner.

Please don't. But the words Sadie longed to say turned to mush in her head. She shot a glance at Nora and wondered if her sister's face might burst into flames, the way it beamed red in the shadow of the streetlight. Silly girl had a crush on Reed Harris.

It worried Sadie to think she might have a small one, as well.

Chapter Five

After singing Christmas carols around the decorated tree, Reed followed the Swanson clan to the church for refreshments. Sadie, Nora, and Miranda led the group, the younger children bantering among themselves as they trailed, and Reed and Paul brought up the rear, discussing everything from farming to wheat prices to business at the livery. Daniel had gone off with some school friends, no doubt to chase girls. It hadn't been all that many years ago that Reed had done the same. In fact, not much had changed since then, for as Paul talked, Reed found himself distracted by the sight of Sadie's black hair cascading down her back, her camel-colored coat making quite a contrast. He was like a schoolboy himself. Pathetic.

The ladies from the church stood behind long serving tables, passing out cookies and tins of hot cocoa. All around, laughter and friendly chatter filled the frigid night. The air held a bite cold enough to make it appear as though dozens of folks, including children, were smoking nicotine sticks, when in fact it was their breaths creating the great white puffs. For that reason, nobody stood still for any period of time. It was just too cold to linger in one spot. A friend of Paul's approached and began conversing with him, so Reed took the opportunity to bid him a good evening and slip away to mingle with the crowd, meanwhile keeping an eye on Sadie and trying to work up the nerve to talk to her. He didn't want to make a pest of himself, but at the same time, there were other eligible bachelors in and around Little Hickman. That thought alone nearly pushed him into panic mode and gave him the pluck he needed to approach her. She'd been engaged in conversation with an older woman, and as soon as the lady walked away, he stepped in.

"Evening, Sadie. It's the first chance I've gotten to really speak a few words to you."

She whirled on her heel and rewarded him with a smile. "Oh, hello, Mr. Harris."

"Reed."

"Reed. Sorry, I keep forgetting." She clasped her gloved hands in front of her, apparently having already finished her hot cocoa. "Thank you for rescuing Jacob Michael. That boy is easily distracted, and the worst part is, few things worry him."

"No need to thank me. It gave me the chance to officially meet your family." He rubbed his hands together, wishing he'd slipped on some gloves. "It sure is a cold one." Why did folks always use weather as a fallback topic of conversation?

"Yes, it almost feels like it could snow again, although when has it ever snowed twice before Christmas?" She shivered.

"Never that I can recall." He continued brushing his hands together. "Would you mind if I walked you back to your apartment—when you're ready to leave, that is?"

He'd braced himself for her rejection, so it surprised him when she answered, "Thank you for the offer. I'm ready to leave right now, actually."

"Excellent." Slightly breathless, he made a loop with his arm, and she actually put her hand through. When they started to walk, a chipper voice prompted both of them to stop and turn.

"Sadie, there you are! We've been looking for you." Liza Broughton hurried in her direction, accompanied by Emma Atkins, and Sadie quickly extricated her hand from Reed's arm.

Emma smiled at Reed before addressing Sadie. "Liza and I are directing the children's Christmas program this year, and we were wondering if…well, we were hoping you might be willing to help."

Sadie's open palm went promptly to her chest. "Help? Me? Oh, but I don't—"

"We promise we won't work you too hard," Emma assured her. "We just need assistance corralling all the youngsters at practice and helping them to learn the songs and their parts."

"I'm directing the choir, accompanied on piano by Bess Barrington," Liza said, "and Emma is organizing the program and doing the narration and such." She leaned in closer. "It'll be fun. Promise."

Reed did a quick search of Sadie's face for some enthusiasm, but he couldn't find any.

"You're a seamstress, aren't you?" Liza prodded her.

"Yes, but—"

"Well, we could surely use some help stitchin' costumes," said Emma. "A few ladies will be workin' together over in my boardinghouse dining room next Monday night if you'd care to join them. The costumes are nothing elaborate, mind you, so it won't be difficult. You know the saying, 'Many hands make work go faster'—or some such thing. It made sense the first time I heard it."

Sadie actually giggled. "'Many hands make light work.' It's a proverb of John Heywood."

"There, you see?" Emma beamed. "You've already talked yourself into it."

"Nora is singing a solo in the program," Liza told her. "Did you know that?"

Sadie released a small gasp. "Nora? No, she never said a word to me."

"Well, I gave her the music just a few days ago, so perhaps she hasn't had a chance to work on it yet. We've also selected Margaret Swain and Jacob Michael to play the parts of Mary and Joseph."

"Really? Jacob Michael is playing Joseph?" Sadie bit her lip. "Are you sure? He can be a bit…distracted."

Emma smiled. "We have every confidence he'll do a fine job."

"What is Nora singing?" Sadie asked.

"'What Child Is This?'" Emma said. "Your stepmother promised to help her learn it."

Sadie nodded. "Miranda is good with the children. She'll see that she learns it well."

Emma touched Sadie's arm. "And we thought that if you helped with the program, your presence at the practices would give her a boost of confidence."

Sadie sighed. "When are the practices?"

"Next Tuesday and Thursday from seven to eight," Liza replied. "The children took their music home with them after Sunday school two weeks ago and are to be practicing the songs."

Sadie inhaled deeply, as if they had asked of her a life-altering task and not just two nights of Christmas program practice.

"I suppose I could do that," she said with a nod. "Yes, I'll help."

Was it his imagination, or did the other ladies just breathe a joint sigh of relief?

"It appears you've been cornered into volunteering," Reed said to Sadie as they strolled back toward the center of town. "How do you feel about that?"

"Well, I could hardly turn them down after learning that my brother and sister are playing key parts in the program," Sadie said. "I have to tell you, though, I'm not a big fan of Christmas. Not like I used to be."

He kicked a pebble out of the way and stuffed his hands in his pockets. She never had taken his arm again, even though he'd made another loop in invitation after Liza and Emma had left. "I sort of figured that."

"The memories...."

"I imagine they go deep." There was an awkward pause, and he pondered how to proceed without sounding like he believed he had all the answers. "Have you thought about making new memories?"

"New memories?"

"Yes. You don't have to spend your life living in the past, Sadie. You can start making fresh memories. Good ones."

She frowned. "I don't live in the past. I'm doing my best to move forward."

Annoyance lined her tone—the very response he'd wanted to avoid evoking. Still, maybe she needed a challenge. "I'd like to escort you on a real outing sometime, Sadie. By 'real outing,' I mean taking you to dinner or to a play in Lexington, or even just inviting you to sit with me in church some Sunday and then maybe going for a buggy ride afterward and stopping somewhere along the banks of the creek for a picnic."

Their footsteps on the wooden sidewalk pierced the air, blending with the clip-clop of horses' hooves in the distance. "A picnic in December doesn't sound too appealing," she finally said.

He gave a light laugh. "You're right, picnics are better suited for springtime—when the forsythia is in bloom and the daffodils are just opening."

She glanced at him. "I didn't have you figured for one familiar with flowers."

He grinned. "I love flowers. I aim to plant a garden this spring, with both flowers and vegetables. I'm a man of many talents, my lady." He paused to gesture with a silly bow, relieved to have earned a smile out of her.

"I love gardens. Unfortunately, it's kind of hard planting one on rental property. I'm fortunate enough that Mr. Bordon allows me free use of his horse and buggy whenever the need arises."

"Feel free to help me with mine if you ever get the hankering to get your hands dirty."

She gave a little nod and another smile but didn't say anything, and he feared their dialog had met a snag. Since Reed deliberately walked at a leisurely pace, a few fellow citizens passed them, some carrying little ones, others exchanging excited chatter about the events of the evening and the prettily decorated tree in plain view for all to see. The town lamplighter, Luke Newman, with his father's help, had fashioned temporary posts on all four sides of the tree with flame-lit glass globes to shine upward so that all could enjoy its regal beauty by night. Indeed, it made a lovely sight.

When they reached the bakery door, Sadie started fishing in her coat pocket for her key. Icy air sent a chill through the length of Reed as he scrambled for a way to rekindle the conversation. Frosty temperatures didn't usually bother him—nothing warm about the livery in December—but his nerves exacerbated the effect of the cold.

"I meant what I said about the real date, Sadie. Sometime—when you're ready, that is. I guess those first two outings, if you can call them 'outings,' were a little premature."

She looked down at her boots, the toe peeking out from beneath her long skirt, then shifted her weight and cleared her throat. "I...I don't know how to make myself ready, Reed."

"What do you mean?"

"I mean, maybe I'm a little...I don't know...."

"Scared?"

When she lifted her head, she looked at the starry sky instead of at him. Tears had filled her eyes, and he felt like a rotten heel for having put them there. She expelled a loud breath and dropped her shoulders, eyes still gazing overhead. "I'm a widow, Reed. To be honest, I can't see why you'd want to associate with me."

He couldn't help it; he cupped her cheeks with both hands and dabbed at her tears with both thumbs. "Why would you say that?"

She looked him head-on. "Have you ever been married?" she asked soberly.

"No, of course not. But what does that have to do—"

"We have nothing in common."

"Sure we do. In fact, I bet we have more things in common than either of us even knows about, the main and most important thing being our relationship with God. I bet all it would take is a little exploring, and we'd discover a whole host of other—"

"No." She encircled his wrists with her fingers and pushed them away, then stepped back. "I still think about my husband every day."

Her words struck him like a hammer to the gut. "I'm not trying to make you forget him." Or was he? He surely didn't want to fall in love with someone who couldn't love him back with every part of her being. Blast it all! How did one compete with a dead husband?

She unlocked her door, pushed it open, and stepped over the threshold. Inside, she turned to face him, gloved hand squeezing the door.

A wave of desperation washed over him to keep her talking to him for just a few more minutes. "We can take it slow," he murmured. Saints and souls, if he wasn't groveling.

"Good night, Reed. And thank you again for seeing me home." She closed the door and turned the lock, and he felt the hard click right in his chest.

"Oh, Lord," he whispered while watching through the window glass as she moved to the rear of the bakery. Without so much as a backward glance to see if he was still there, she disappeared from view. "Help her, Lord. Help her to look beyond herself and find a brand-new joy in living." He stared into the bakery, where a single gas lamp at the back provided dim light. "What am I doing, God? Am I just playing with fire? She's about as interested in me as I am in a wilted turnip."

Give her time, My son. It was the first time he'd actually sensed an inner nudge from the Spirit to continue with his pursuit, and it gave him an immeasurable sense of peace.

He turned around and headed back to his own little place on Elm Street, more determined now than ever. In the stone-cold night, he took up humming one of the Christmas carols they'd sung as a group around the tree, every breath creating a vaporous white puff.

Chapter Six

Sunday morning didn't promise sunshine, if Sadie's first glimpse out the window was an accurate prediction. She held back the sheer curtain in her tiny living room and peered down at the lifeless street. Nothing moved, save for a few scraps of paper blown by the wind, and the branches of the Christmas tree, which danced gently in the breeze. The men had done a fine job of securing it to the sturdy wood stand and then pounding long stakes deep into the ground around the tree at about the six-foot diameter mark. From each stake, they'd strung a long piece of twine that they'd then wrapped around the trunk to further stabilize the tree from all sides. It would take a very strong wind to knock it off kilter. Some of the ornaments might be in jeopardy, but Sadie doubted that anyone but Iris Winthrop had donated anything of great value. The woman had made a point of announcing that she'd paid a full ten dollars for the tree topper. The amount had drawn a few gasps from folks within earshot. Who in her right mind would pay such an extravagant amount for an ornament to adorn an outdoor tree? Of course, everyone knew the answer to that question.

Sadie donned her best heavy cotton red dress with the tight-fitting bodice, its full skirt gathered into a flattering point in the front and back. The rounded neck and velvet collar provided extra warmth, a welcome feature that warded off the draft coming through the windows across the room. She wished Mr. Bordon would come a little earlier on Sunday mornings to stoke the coal furnace; but even if he did, she supposed it wouldn't make much of a difference, considering how little heat drifted up through the registers in the apartment floor. She crossed the room to her divan and studied her reflection in the wall mirror above it, then secured the chain of her mother's ruby-red Australian crystal pendant behind her neck. Next, she scuttled stocking-footed across the room to where she kept her trunk of shoes, boots, hats, and other paraphernalia. She would need to dress extra warmly today, so, upon shuffling through her choices, she reached for her black Lady Elizabeth lace-up boots. They weren't especially heavy, but they would serve their purpose with the use of her long wool socks, which, of course, would be hidden from view. Last, with her hair drawn up in a braided bun suitable for church attendance, she removed the lid of a hatbox and retrieved her gray wool felt bonnet with the matching gloves. Her long gray coat, with substantial silver buttons, would finish the look.

She wouldn't bother with her pendant watch, but she did pick it up from the tiny china saucer on the sofa stand to check the time. It read quarter to ten—past time for heading briskly down the sidewalk toward the white clapboard building known as Little Hickman Community Church.

When at last she stepped into the street, something quite startling struck her. That morning was the first time she hadn't awakened with Tom on her mind. Instead, the crazy question as to whether she might happen upon Mr. Reed Harris at church had been the first thing to enter her head—preposterous, considering she'd made it quite plain to him a few days ago she had no interest in being courted by him. *Pfff*, she thought. *I am such a tweedle-head. I don't know what on earth I want.*

You should want Me above all others. Her steps halted almost of their own accord, and she looked upward, as if to seek out the voice she'd heard so clearly. Hearing nothing further, she resumed her steps. "Lord," she whispered, "I realize I've failed to place my trust fully in You. Help me to find my way back to You."

When Sadie arrived at church at two minutes to ten, few empty seats remained, as had become the norm thanks to the Reverend Atkins' fine preaching. Her family usually saved a spot for her, but this morning, it looked as though she'd been crowded out by another couple. She had to search for a moment before she spotted an available place, at the end of the fifth pew from the back, right next to a drafty window. She vowed never again to spend so much time trying to figure out what to wear on Sunday morning. That ought to be a task for Saturday night. And what did it matter, anyway, what she wore, as long as she looked presentable? She'd taken extra time with her hair that morning, preened a trifle longer than usual in front of the mirror, and even applied a bit of color to her cheeks. She ought to be ashamed. Getting ready for church should have next to nothing to do with primping and everything to do with preparing her heart to worship God. She would do well to remind herself of that next Sunday.

Once she had situated herself on the bench, Liza Broughton leaned over, stretched a hand across two youngsters, and touched her arm. "Good morning, Sadie," she whispered with a bright smile. "Good to see you on this cold December morning. Don't forget about Tuesday night's practice for the Christmas program!"

Sadie smiled and nodded, and then Mr. Burton, one of the song leaders, approached the podium and announced the first hymn, "O For a Thousand Tongues to Sing." She turned to page 231 in her hymnal, biting back a bigger smile. Ever since moving to Little Hickman, she hadn't been able to sing this song without thinking about Iris Winthrop and her wagging tongue, and she wondered if others in the sanctuary thought the same. She glanced about but saw nary an indication of it, which made her berate herself for not giving God her full focus. Worse, while permitting her eyes to scan the crowd, she spied the back of Reed Harris's head, with his coffee-colored hair, and her stomach took one of those strange flips. Oh, for the love of all things sacred, what was wrong with her? She had her heart fully under control, and no man, no matter that he had the broadest shoulders in all of Little Hickman, or that he had a smile capable of melting an ice cube, would upturn her cart of neatly arranged emotions.

The sermon tugged mightily at her heart. The reverend spoke of letting go of life's hurts and finding new purpose, of learning to depend on Christ for strength and courage, and of moving forward to lead the kind of life that draws others to the Savior.

He talked about the Christmas season being one of giving and *forgiving*, and encouraged the congregants to lay down their own cares and worries and to try putting others' needs ahead of their own. "Joy is not so much an emotion as it is an act," the reverend said, his words yanking at her very essence like an anchor pulling a boat to an abrupt stop before dangerous waters. "Happiness is the emotion," he said. "The temptation is to grumble and complain, but did you know that God's Word instructs us to be joyful in spite of our circumstances? It is an active decision we must make in obedience to God's commands. I'm not saying that He intends us to leap with gladness when we lose our farms, our means of income, a loved one, or the very clothes on our back. Not at all. What I am saying is that it is very possible to maintain our sense of joy in the midst of dark times—just like the apostle Paul, who said, '*I have learned, in whatsoever state I am, therewith to be content.*'"

Reverend Atkins also cited Psalm 118:24: "*This is the day which the LORD hath made; we will rejoice and be glad in it.*"

"What will you do with this day, my friends?" he challenged them. "Will you wallow in your adverse circumstances, complaining about them? Or might you choose to rise above them and rejoice? If you bear in mind that the present burden you carry isn't yours alone but also God's, it makes the going so much easier."

Her inclination was to rebel against the whole notion of rejoicing in unfortunate circumstances, but there was also a deeper part that longed to lay it all down—if only she could. Did God truly expect her to thank Him for stealing away her young groom? Hadn't He done her an injustice by taking him? Did He now want her to thank Him for that? *I don't know, Lord. I don't know what You want from me.*

All of you, My child. I want all of you.

But that meant relinquishment, and she didn't know if she could do that, either—surrender all her hurts, fears, and disappointments.

You can do all things through Christ who strengthens you. The quiet assurance from Philippians helped her drink deeply of its timeless truth and fight back her tears.

After the benediction, folks began buttoning coats, securing scarves, and donning winter hats. No new snow had fallen, but it might as well have, as bitter as the air had turned over the past several days. Reed let his eyes roam the crowd of worshippers. Several waved or nodded from afar, but the person he truly longed to see, a woman with glistening brown eyes and charcoal hair, hadn't come to church that day—at least, he hadn't seen her in her usual spot with her family.

He moved out into the aisle and began to head toward the front entrance, where Reverend Jon and Emma stood, ready to greet the congregants.

"Reed. Nice to see you again, lad."

He turned at the male voice from behind. "Mr. Swanson." He nodded. "Nice to see you, as well." He couldn't recall the last time someone had referred to him as "lad." With Paul were his wife, Miranda; the youngest, Elizabeth, who held her stepmother's hand; and Nora, Jacob Michael, and Daniel. They all greeted him with friendly smiles. They were a good-looking bunch, and he'd liked them all immediately. "Mrs. Swanson, nice to see you, too—and the rest of you. Fine service this morning, wasn't it?"

Miranda returned a broad smile, revealing one crooked front tooth, which neither added to nor detracted from her appearance. In fact, her finely crafted attire fully made up for any physical flaws. He noticed how nicely all the children were dressed, too, and figured she had much to do with it. "Indeed, both inspiring and convicting."

"I have to agree."

His eyes came to rest on a very mesmerized-looking Nora. "And how are you this morning, young lady?"

She gave a tiny curtsy, fingertips clutching a bit of fabric on either side. "Fine, thank you."

Reed grinned, turning his hat in his hands. "You look as pretty as a flower today."

She blushed. "Thank you." She certainly resembled her older sister, with her long, flowing hair and dark eyes. He wanted to ask after Sadie's whereabouts, but he didn't want to betray his keen interest in her. "Well, you folks enjoy your Sabbath," was all he said.

He started to turn, but then Paul stopped him with a firm grip on his shoulder. "Say, how would you like to join us for Sunday dinner?"

His wife's face brightened. "Oh, what a lovely idea. We always have plenty! Do come."

"We live over the creek in a big ol' farmhouse a short distance from the Bergens' place," Paul added. "You'll pass Ben and Liza Broughton's farm first, then the Bergens'."

"I've been out that way, yes, but I…well, I don't want to infringe on your Sunday."

"Not at all," Miranda said. "We love Sunday visitors." She leaned in closer. "We're having roast beef and potatoes, if that will help sway you."

"And apple pie, which I baked myself," Nora added, standing taller.

Reed laughed. "Believe me, I don't need convincing." There was always the chance Sadie would be there. Would she resent the intrusion, especially after making it clear she had no interest in him? He decided it best not to bring her up. "What time would you like me?"

Paul reached for his pocket watch and gave it a glance. "How does one o'clock sound?"

Reed nodded. "I'll see you then. Much obliged."

Sadie always looked forward to Sunday dinners with her family. After today's sermon and her narrow escape from a batch of tears, she'd chosen to make a fast getaway after the preacher's final amen. She'd beaten everyone else to the door, including the reverend and Emma, and had scurried down the sidewalk back to her apartment before anyone had a chance to say hello. Her family probably thought she'd missed the service. Spending time with them today would make for a nice diversion, something she sorely needed.

The ride to the Swanson farm was cold but refreshing. Rather than hitch Mr. Bordon's roan, Charlie, to the wagon, she'd decided to saddle him up. It may not have been the most ladylike thing to do on the Sabbath, but the desire to feel the wind in her face outweighed her better judgment. She rode fast and hard for the first five minutes, her hair coming undone and her skirts flaring, then took pity on poor old Charlie and slowed the pace. It wouldn't do for him to arrive in a lather in this weather and catch his death. Mr. Bordon would never forgive her. When she reached the family farm, her head felt clearer, her emotions more controlled. Good. Now she could sit with her family at the table and enjoy senseless blather and good-natured laughter, and no one would guess it was all a front.

When she dismounted in front of the rambling farmhouse, she noted an unfamiliar rig parked outside but thought little of it. Her father had a habit of inviting new couples or young families to Sunday dinner. She would have preferred not having to make conversation with strangers, but then she recalled how the reverend had encouraged everyone to show a generous Christmas spirit to others, and she checked herself. Best to lay aside her selfish desires and put others' needs ahead of her own. Hadn't he said something to that effect?

After she'd looped Charlie's reins over the post a couple of times, the front door flew open. "Sadie!" Nora hissed in a strange voice, running across the porch to meet her. "You didn't come to church. Where were you?"

"Yes, I did. I just came in a little late and left a little early. Why are you so flushed?"

"We have company!" If another of her siblings had spoken in such a high-pitched voice, Sadie might have been alarmed, but Nora was emotional by nature.

"Yes, I saw the rig. What family did Papa bring home with him this time? And why aren't you inside entertaining the children?"

"He didn't bring a family." She lowered her voice and leaned in close, her eyes having rounded like two brown boulders. "It's *him.*"

"*Him?*" As soon as she voiced the question, the answer came to her, and a knot balled up in her stomach while she waited for the confirmation.

"That liveryman. Oh, my living, breathing stars, Sadie. He is like a vision. Have you ever seen anyone so good-looking? Well, I mean, other than your Tom, of course."

"What is he doing here?"

"Papa invited him. We were standing around talking at church, and Papa just up and asked him to come out. He didn't accept right off, mind you, but when I told him I'd baked an apple pie, why, that took care of his hesitation. I'm sure that's what did it. He told me I looked as pretty as a flower, Sadie. Ain't that something?"

"Isn't, you mean. And don't forget what I told you about looking at boys and men at your age. Great heavens, I think you and I need to have a talk soon."

"About what? Kissing?"

"Nora Swanson!" Sadie planted her hands on her hips. "What do you know about kissing?"

"Only what it feels like from my end. I've been practicing on my pillow."

Few people were as frank as Nora, and sometimes the things she said made Sadie laugh out loud. She held back this time.

"Well, see to it you keep it that way—at least for the next few years." She removed her gloves and stared at the house for ten long seconds, debating whether to stay and brave it out or get back on Charlie and retreat to safety.

"You look rather a mess, Sadie. What happened to your hair?"

"Oh." She clutched her mass of locks with both hands. "I am a disaster, aren't I? Oh, dear."

"I wouldn't worry." Nora smiled. "Mr. Harris didn't come to see you, anyways. It was Papa who invited 'im."

"Oh. Well, that's true enough." For crying in a bucket! What difference did it make the condition in which she arrived for Sunday dinner? She wasn't out to impress Reed Harris. She'd made it good and clear the other night that she hadn't yet gotten over the loss of her departed husband. Chances were good Reed wouldn't stay much past dessert, and if he did, well, she'd just leave ahead of him. Yes, that was exactly what she'd do.

Chapter Seven

Sadie didn't shower him with cordiality, and Reed couldn't blame her. After all, his presence at her family's table must have shocked her. It made him almost regret having come, but then, he hadn't known for sure she'd even be here. How was he to know she visited her family every Sunday for dinner? Moreover, how did one turn down a dinner invitation without a legitimate excuse? *"Sorry, but I'm having bread and butter for Sunday lunch"*? She was a stubborn thing; he'd give her that—and about as aloof as a cat right now. Nora, on the other hand, had an engaging way about her that made conversing at the table a delight.

"Remember that time Daniel fell off Oscar, and Papa had to rescue him from the pen? He thought Oscar was a horse."

"Well, he was big enough to be one." Daniel looked at Reed. "Oscar was our hog."

"Oh." Reed chuckled as he pictured the episode. "How old were you?"

"It was last year," Nora put in.

Daniel rolled his eyes. "No, it wasn't, squirt. I was only three or four, and you were just a baby, so you don't even remember it."

"I've heard about it plenty of times, so I feel like I saw it firsthand."

"You never should have been in there," Paul said, in between bites of tender beef. "That beast could've killed you."

"What happened to Oscar?" Jacob Michael asked.

"We ate 'im, dummy," answered Daniel.

"Ate 'im? Did we really, Papa?"

"Well, you didn't, since you weren't around then."

"Why don't we get another hog like Oscar?" Jacob Michael wanted to know, talking with his mouth full.

His father scowled. "Because I'm afraid you'd do the same thing Daniel did—climb right in there with him."

"No, I wouldn't. I ain't that dumb. I know a horse from a hog."

"Let's change the subject, shall we?" said Miranda. She dabbed her mouth with her napkin, lowered it to her lap, and directed her attention to Reed. "Mr. Harris, tell us a bit about yourself."

"Yes, tell us everything," said Nora, seeming to have lost her inhibitions around him. Reed couldn't help but shoot a quick glance at Sadie. She'd barely eaten a thing, while every other plate was nearly cleared. Good golly, had he ruined her appetite?

"There's not much to tell, I'm afraid."

"Of course there is," Miranda insisted. "Do you have siblings? Where do they live? And what of your parents?"

He quickly caught them up on the sister who had passed, his married brother living in South Carolina, and his mother and stepfather living in Chattanooga.

"Will you be spending Christmas with them?" she asked.

"No, afraid not, but it's perfectly fine. I'm accustomed to spending the holiday alone. I'm sure to be busy at the livery, anyway."

"Well, you'll at least have Christmas dinner with us," Paul insisted.

The invitation caught Reed off guard. Out of the corner of his eye, he observed Sadie's head shoot straight up. How was he to keep his distance from her if her family kept inviting him to join them? He couldn't possibly accept and then violate her rightful place with her own family. "I'll have to give that some thought, but I do appreciate the offer. It'll all depend on how busy I am at the livery." Now he'd just have to make sure to be extra busy.

"How'd you happen to buy the livery?" Daniel asked.

"Well, my grandfather offered it to me summer before last. It took me some time to pray about it and then weigh the pros and cons. When I felt confident it'd be a smart move on my part, I started gathering up my funds. I made the transition a little over a year ago."

"And you have no regrets?" Paul asked him.

"None, sir. I've enjoyed it more than I ever thought possible."

"Excellent."

"Do you gots a wife?" young Elizabeth asked.

"Uh, nope. Never had one," he said, taking up his glass of water for a couple of long swallows.

Elizabeth glanced at Sadie. "My sister had a husband, but he died."

The room fell silent, awkwardly so, and Sadie's lack of a reply made it all the more uncomfortable.

"Yes, I…I heard that," said Reed, hating that he'd stumbled. "And I'm very sorry."

"I can't hardly 'member it," said Elizabeth. "Sometimes I lay in bed at night and try to 'member, but it don't come back to me."

"Elizabeth," said Miranda, her voice sounding rushed, "why don't you come help me cut the pie? And Nora, you clear the table."

Nora started to stand, but Sadie pushed her chair back ahead of her and rose. "No need. I'll do it."

"I'll help," Nora said.

That left the men and boys sitting there. Reed laid his silverware atop his plate and set his napkin on the table next to it. Without a word, Sadie added it to the stack she had already gathered and disappeared into the kitchen.

"Never can tell what's going to come out of that young'un's mouth," Paul said in an apologetic tone. "Tom's passing is still a touchy subject."

"Sadie'd do well to talk more about it, Papa," said Daniel, sounding more like a man than a boy of fifteen.

"I agree, Son, but you can't force these things." He glanced at Reed. "Don't know if you've heard much about the sawmill accident."

He nodded slowly. "I heard some, yes, and it must have been a terrible thing for all of you, but especially Sadie. I've been praying for her. Only God can heal a broken heart."

"Isn't that the truth?" Paul shook his head. "I lost my wife a few years back and thought I'd never manage without her, especially since I had a whole band of youngsters to raise. But then He brought Miranda into our lives, and she's fit in real well."

"She's pretty decent as mothers go," said Daniel, a twinkle in his eye.

"Yeah, she's nice," said Jacob Michael. "I wished I could 'member my real mother better, though."

"I wish you could, as well, Son. She was a fine woman." Paul took a swig of water, then furrowed his brow, as if weighing his next words. "She may not appear so, Reed, but Sadie is a strong woman. You'd do well to get to know her better."

He couldn't help but smile. "Don't think I haven't tried, sir, but I don't think the feelings are mutual. Matter of fact, I don't think she's all that pleased about my being here right now."

"Sadie's had a rough go of it, but it's time she started living again."

"She's too scared," Daniel said.

Reed blinked twice at the boy's immense insight.

"What's she scared about?" asked Jacob Michael.

"I'll tell you later, squirt," Daniel said. "It ain't nothin' for you to worry about."

Paul passed Reed a sly grin across the table and lifted one eyebrow. "Might be you're the one to ease her fears. You'd have my blessing."

He could hardly believe it. Didn't most men have to work hard to win a father's approval? "Well, I appreciate that vote of confidence, sir, but your daughter doesn't appear too interested in me."

"We'll see. Give her time, son."

Hmm. Interesting that Reed had sensed his heavenly Father implanting those same words in his head just the other night.

No sooner had Paul made the remark than Miranda, Nora, Elizabeth, and Sadie came out of the kitchen, each one carrying two plates of a slice of apple pie topped with a dollop of vanilla ice cream. Reed's taste buds started doing a little dance.

Elizabeth walked the slowest of all, guarding her plates like her life depended on it. "I get t' serve Mr. Reed," she announced.

"All right, you serve him and Daniel. How's that?" Miranda asked.

"No, I'll serve Mr. Reed and Papa."

"Suit yourself, then," Miranda said, winking across the room at Reed.

He grinned back, then took up his napkin again and spread it across his lap.

He chanced a look at Sadie and inwardly smiled. She showed no interest in exchanging glances, but he wouldn't let that deter him. He had her father and her brother on his side.

Conversation picked up again during dessert, and Sadie finally felt herself relaxing. Everyone contributed, especially Daniel and Nora, who seemed to want to share one story after another. Most of their tales did prove quite entertaining. If Nora had been shy before, she'd lost all her reticence and now took apparent delight in revealing her animated personality. Sadie could not help but steal a few quick glimpses at Reed, being careful to avoid eye contact. Mustn't give him—or her family—the impression that she found him the least bit attractive, especially when she didn't want to admit it even to herself.

"Sadie, tell about the time you an' ol' Wilma the cow had a run-in with…well, you know," Daniel urged.

"What?" Sadie jerked to life. "No, you've all heard that story plenty of times." Everyone had just recovered from laughing about the time her father had neglected to remove the horse from the stall he was mucking. The old boy had gotten a little tired of her father's company and had decided to shove him up against the wall, making him lose his balance and landing him face-first in the wheelbarrow full of manure.

"Mr. Harris ain't heard it," said Daniel.

The heat of a blush crept up her neck. Until now, she'd managed to stay in the background of the conversation, keeping her laughter to a few chuckles. These were tales that tended to come out whenever someone new joined them for Sunday dinner. Normally, she didn't mind the retelling, but today, she'd sooner sit and listen than repeat her own silly story for the hundredth time, no matter that Reed Harris hadn't heard it.

Reed adjusted his position in the dining chair and quirked an eyebrow at her. "This I have to hear."

She lifted one shoulder. "There's not much to tell."

"Yes there is, Sadie-girl," her father said with a smile. "You always tell it well."

Sadie-girl. Even though she was a widowed woman, her father still called her by the pet name he'd given her long before she'd had any siblings.

She took a hurried sip of water and swallowed. "Well, all right, then. It was an early summer morning, a Sunday, and I got up, dressed, and went out to the barn in the dark. I carried a lantern, but I recall the moon being full and bright. I'd heard Papa say the night before that he planned to sleep in an extra hour. Since milking Wilma was my job, I decided to get started earlier than usual. Everyone else was sleeping, of course; but, unbeknownst to me, Daniel had gotten up, dressed, and gone out to the barn ahead of me. He was about ten, and I was probably twenty-one or twenty-two. I don't recall, exactly, but it was when we were still living in Frankfort.

"Anyway, I went to the barn, and the first thing I noticed was a low-burning lantern hanging on a hook. This I found slightly odd, but then I figured Papa must have decided to come out early, after all, and had left it there for me. The next thing I noticed was that Wilma had somehow turned herself around in her stall so that she had her backside to me, and she wasn't moving so much as a single hair. I didn't want to sneak up on her, for fear of spooking her, so I just made a little shuffling noise on the concrete floor, thinking that would bring her out of her stupor. It didn't work. She just kept on staring straight ahead, intently focused on something. I decided to ignore her strange behavior and went about gathering my stool and pail. I opened the gate and sidled in next to her. She was so used to my comings and goings that she hardly seemed to notice when I entered. I set the stool down and started talking to her in that way I always did when I situated myself next to her. She finally acknowledged me, but she wasn't herself. That's when I heard a tiny whisper coming from the stall next to me and saw a single eye peering through a knothole. 'Sadie, don't move,' the voice said. Daniel's, of course."

Giggles started erupting even before she reached the clincher, and when she glanced up at Reed, she caught him in a fully mesmerized state, eyes popping, mouth sagging slightly open.

"Naturally, I moved," she continued. "I mean, he startled me, for heaven's sake!"

More riotous giggles.

"I jumped off the stool and started to scold Daniel for scaring me." She shook her head. "Foolish reaction on my part."

Now her father's booming laughter caused his round belly to bump against the table, jiggling the water glasses. Everyone but Reed knew what was coming.

"My sudden response brought Wilma to life, and she started doing a regular jig before letting out a ghastly moo. Her hind leg came out and shoved me—hard—knocking me right off my feet. Pretty soon, a black-and-white cat sauntered past my head. At least, I thought it was a cat—until it lifted its tail at me and hit me with a warm spray that drizzled down my arm. I screamed, Daniel started crying, Wilma mooed clear to the moon, the chickens all set to squawking, and the goats kicked up a regular storm in their pens. Thankfully, the horses were out to pasture, or I think they would've knocked down the walls."

"You were skunked!" Reed said before he joined the laughing spree.

"Was I ever! I skipped church, of course, and took a bath that lasted at least six hours."

"Which didn't help a bit," her father said.

"She stunk to high heaven!" Daniel giggled.

"As did Wilma, since he got part of her leg," Sadie put in. "Unfortunately, I took the brunt of the attack."

"Holy crow!" Reed held a hand to his forehead. "What did you do?"

"She stayed home for two solid weeks and kept scrubbing herself till her skin practically came off," her father supplied.

"Um, I'm almost afraid to ask, but what happened to the skunk?" Reed asked.

"That's anybody's guess," Sadie said. "I think we traumatized him so much, he took off for greener pastures, so to speak."

"Or Papa took him down to the creek for a swim," said Daniel.

Sadie laughed. "Daniel, you always say that, but I don't think Papa dared go near that critter." She looked at her father. "You didn't, did you?"

He raised his eyebrows. "Some things are better left a mystery."

After that, the conversation began winding down. The women began clearing the table while the menfolk stretched. Jacob Michael and Elizabeth put on their winter gear and went outside to play, and the family dog—a half-deaf, mostly blind yellow lab named Rubin, who rarely ventured outside—lay sprawled in front of the fireplace, oblivious to everything and everyone. Outside, the wind gusted around the house, hooting like a high-pitched owl.

"Mr. Harris is so nice—and handsome, to boot," Nora said as she dried a plate with a red-checkered towel. Sadie helped dry, too, while Miranda washed, though Sadie would have bet her towel was three times wetter than Nora's, the way the girl went on, stopping between dishes to stare off into space. "You oughtta go for him, Sadie."

"Oh, for crying in a washtub, Nora! You've been kissing your pillow way too often."

"Kissing her pillow?" Miranda stopped washing and gaped at Sadie.

"That's how I practice, Miranda," Nora said simply.

"Practice *kissing?*"

"Sure. You and Papa kiss, don't you?"

"Nora Marie, that is none of your business," Sadie scolded.

"Well, of course we do." Miranda went back to washing, perhaps a bit more vigorously this time. "When you fall in love, Nora, the kissing part comes naturally. But you have years before you need to start worrying about that, do you hear me? Years."

Nora's lips drooped in a pout. "I know, but I can at least think about it so I'll be ready when the time comes, can't I?"

"I suppose."

"Nora, you are fixin' to turn my hair gray," Sadie told her, meaning it. "You're growing up too fast."

"She surely is," said Miranda.

Around half past three, Reed announced his departure, thanking everyone for the delicious food, lovely company, and lively conversation. Sadie had been waiting for him to leave so that she could follow suit a half hour or so later.

"Why don't you two ride back together?" her father suggested.

She cast him a glare. She didn't need him playing Mr. Matchmaker.

"That'd be up to Sadie, sir," Reed was kind enough to say. Still, how could she wriggle her way out of it, since she really was ready to leave? She hesitated only a moment. Oh, bother. What could it hurt?

"I suppose that'd be fine," she finally said. "Just let me get my wrap."

Chapter Eight

No question, Reed found Sadie downright irresistible, and spending the afternoon with her family today had cemented the attraction. He wanted to pursue her—shoot, chase her, even! At the same time, he knew he had to be cautious in how he went about it. Sadie Bennett wasn't just any woman. Saints and souls! He knew as much about charming her as he knew about lassoing a kangaroo. Oh, it wasn't that he lacked skill. He'd courted plenty of girls in his day—he'd even come close to marrying one a few years back, until he'd realized that her domineering mother intended to move in with them. After that, it hadn't taken him long to bolt. No, it was that Sadie had made herself inaccessible, like a fine piece of china kept on a high shelf, far out of reach.

He parked his rig in front of the bakery, climbed down, and then followed behind Sadie as she rode her horse to the barn out back. As soon as she reached the barn door and pulled on the reins, he stepped up to offer her a hand down. And when she placed her gloved palm in his, his stomach lurched with delight. *Lord, I'm as giddy as a five-year-old who's just had his first spoonful of chocolate pudding.*

They worked together unbridling the horse, putting on its halter, and removing the cinch, saddle, and blanket. Reed hung everything on the wall according to Sadie's instructions.

"I'll wipe and brush him down if you want to check his hooves," she offered.

"Sure," he said, and they continued in a congenial manner, though their conversation was kept to a minimum. The whole process took no more than ten or fifteen minutes, and when they were finished, Sadie led the horse into his stall, turned him around so that he faced her, and then unsnapped the lead rope before stepping out of the stall. Reed pulled the gate closed behind her and latched it, and they walked out of the barn and back down the alley toward the front of the bakery.

"I had a great day," Reed said. "Your family is wonderful."

Sadie smiled. "I did, too. And, yes, they are."

If he was ever going to win her over, he would have to do better than this. "I loved your skunk story," he threw in. "You told it well. By the way, you didn't get hurt, did you? When the cow kicked you backward, I mean?"

She laughed. "Well, thank you for asking. You'll notice my welfare never even came up today. It's been a standard joke for so many years that everyone was so concerned with how badly I stunk, no one even cared if I'd broken an arm or a leg. They just wanted me to move to some far-off country."

He tossed back his head and let out a hearty chuckle. Combined, their laughter made sweet music. He could grow accustomed to this.

"But, no, I wasn't hurt—unless you count my pride," Sadie concluded.

"Well, at least it was just your pride. Pride heals. What was Daniel doing out there, anyway?"

"Good question. He said later that he'd planned to sneak up on me, the scoundrel. I guess it worked."

At the door, she pulled her key out of her coat pocket, then paused before positioning it in the keyhole. "Thank you for accompanying me home. It was…nice."

"It was my pleasure." He would have accepted an invitation upstairs, but he didn't want to press his luck. He did take a moment to study her lips, though, going so far as to imagine what it would be like to kiss them. "You have a nice evening."

"And you, as well."

He took a step back, hands shoved into his pockets. From behind him, his horse whinnied, as if to tell him to get moving.

With a shy smile, she turned, unlocked her door, and then stepped inside. At the window, rather than quickly disappear as she'd done on prior occasions, she smiled through the glass pane and gave a hurried wave. He reciprocated the gesture, then turned and unlooped his horse's reins from the hitching post and quickly mounted. He couldn't help it, he grinned all the way back to the livery.

On Monday evening, after a quick supper, Sadie trudged across the street to Emma's Boardinghouse. Her stomach churned with unaccountable nerves. It wasn't as if she never attended social functions. In addition, she went to church every

Sunday, for goodness' sake; and if that wasn't enough, she worked in an establishment where she had occasion to meet and talk to people every day. Somehow, though, meeting with a group of ladies in a more intimate setting put her on edge. It occurred to her that, much to her chagrin, she'd turned into a regular recluse over the past several months.

As she mounted the boardinghouse steps, she whispered a prayer. "Dear Father, please plant in my spirit a new seed of joy—like the reverend mentioned in his sermon. May Your love light not only *my* path, but also the paths of others. Help me learn to trust more, give more, and love more. Amen."

It was the first such prayer of submission she'd uttered since Tom's death, and right there on the steps of Emma's Boardinghouse, she felt as if a weight had lifted. Oh, she didn't expect never to experience another day of despondency, but something—*Someone*—happened to her in that moment, and it lifted her spirits to new heights.

Gathering a good breath for courage, she rapped on the front door, and within seconds, Emma Atkins opened it and welcomed her inside.

The evening went better than she had expected. It began with introductions. Everyone knew one another, at least on a formal basis, but it proved helpful to Sadie when Emma repeated each one's name. There were eight women in total, a good number for stitching twenty simple costumes.

Sadie sat near one end of Emma's long dining-room table, and the middle-aged widow Fancy Jenkins settled in next to her, pretty near talking her ear off. Sadie didn't mind, though, for it left her no obligation to fill in any pauses. Next to Fancy sat Gladys Hayward, a kindhearted elderly woman, and beside her sat Caroline Warner, a plain yet sweet woman with graying hair and a warm smile. Directly across from Sadie was Iris Winthrop. The woman had curtness down to the letter, which made Sadie wonder why she'd come at all; but then she recalled the comment

Iris had made about not being able to have children, and she wondered if that fact contributed to her vinegary attitude. On either side of Iris sat Frieda Hardy and Bess Barrington.

Emma took her place at the other end of the table, and even then, there was room for more place settings—a good thing, considering the houseful of male boarders who lived there. Even now, a few of them occupied other rooms on the downstairs level, reading, playing cards, or just talking. The reverend himself strolled by at one point, coffee mug in hand, and greeted the ladies, thanking them for helping. On his way to the kitchen, he touched his wife on the shoulder, and she smiled up at him. Their knowing glances created in Sadie an unnamed knot of emotion, but not the sort that brought Tom's image to mind. In truth, she couldn't quite pinpoint the feeling; she knew only that it originated from a need to love and be loved the way the two of them clearly did.

For the next two hours, the women worked, some of them measuring and cutting fabric, making piles of cloth pieces, and stitching together the simple costumes. Others worked on fashioning rope belts to wrap around the loose-fitting garments, and the rest of the women sewed headpieces to coordinate with specific costumes. As was the case with any work bee, there were plenty of things to discuss. The more time that passed, the more relaxed Sadie became, until she found herself contributing to the conversation and laughing along when someone shared a funny story. Fancy Jenkins had a sense of humor that kept things lively. She shared how she used to come to church just to feast her eyes on the handsome preacher, then a bachelor.

"You didn't!" Emma said. "I'm telling him."

Fancy shrugged. "Go ahead. He prob'ly knows it already, since a few of us ladies used to bicker over who would sit in the few front-row seats in Iris's living room. 'Member how we used to hold services in the Winthrops' home till the new building was constructed? Anna Johnson was the worst. She used to try an' beat me to the house just to get that blue velvet chair by the fireplace, which afforded the best view of him."

"Anna Johnson is married with twins!" Bess Barrington exclaimed.

Fancy chuckled. "Didn't matter to her none. Elmer, he stood in the back with the rest of the husbands. Them men, they all knew good an' well their womenfolk were swooning over the preacher. Weren't nothin' they could do about it." She turned her eyes on Emma. "None of us could believe it took you so long to say yes to that man."

"Oh, my stars in heaven!" Emma paused in her stitching to hold her slightly rounded belly and laugh. Apparently, news of her pregnancy had started spreading after the Christmas tree celebration of a week ago. Here, she'd been expecting on the day the selection committee had ridden out to search for the tree, but had anyone suspected it? Sadie surely hadn't, which only reminded her of how self-centered she'd been recently—over the past two years, really.

"Well, I, for one, did not ogle him," Iris Winthrop declared with a sniff. "I recall telling more than one woman how unseemly it was to look upon a man of the cloth in such a manner."

Fancy laughed. "You did scold us a time or two, Iris Winthrop, but I'll be a beakless duck if I didn't catch you flutterin' your eyelashes at him whenever he stopped by the mercantile to purchase somethin'. Why, once I was standin' behind a bolt o' cloth, and I thought you were goin' to swoon when he asked to buy a ball o' twine from you."

This comment provoked a round of laughter.

"Oh, forevermore, I don't recall that." Iris put her hand to her blushing throat.

The reverend came down the stairs and ambled past the ladies, holding up his tin cup. "Time for a refill on my coffee," he announced. "How are the costumes coming along?"

They all stared at him, Emma included, mouths agape.

He stopped to stare back. "What?"

Emma shook her head three times. "Nothing, honey. Nothing at all."

He frowned and scratched his chin. "Well, y'all look as guilty as jailbirds. Did I come in at the wrong time?"

"What? No, 'course not," Bess Barrington said, hiding a smile by lowering her face and concentrating on her stitching.

"Humph." He gave a suspicious half grin. "Perhaps it's one of those things I'd rather not know."

Iris Winthrop cleared her throat. "Yes, perhaps."

He gave a little roll of the eyes and then entered the kitchen. When he disappeared, the women all covered their mouths to conceal their bubbling laughter. Even Iris Winthrop had to stifle a giggle.

Considering they'd spent most of the evening talking, laughing, and nibbling on fresh-baked cookies, the eight of them certainly accomplished a great deal, completing most of the costumes. Fancy offered to finish the remaining ones the next morning at her tailoring shop, Fancy Stitches.

When it came time to leave, the ladies donned their coats and gathered up the few items they'd brought with them. Sadie found herself almost regretting seeing the evening draw to a close. It'd been so long since she'd laughed with a group of ladies, and it placed within her a fierce hunger for more such gatherings.

"Let's get together again soon," Emma suggested to the group, as if reading Sadie's thoughts. "Perhaps we could organize a monthly sewing bee starting in January, to stitch clothes for the less fortunate of Little Hickman. It would be a wonderful way to usher in eighteen ninety-nine, don't you think? Starting out the New Year with mission-minded hearts."

"What a wonderful idea!" Caroline Warner exclaimed.

"You can count me in," said Frieda Hardy.

"And me," Fancy piped up.

"I could donate some fabric," Iris said, after which everyone stood mutely in awe for all of ten seconds.

"That would be mighty generous of you, Iris," Emma finally said. "And we'll extend the opportunity to the rest of the church ladies. We'll start a brand-new church ministry, showing Jesus's love to those who haven't yet experienced it."

Sadie couldn't believe the transformation taking place within her—the excitement stirred up by the prospect of putting others' needs ahead of her own for a change.

"What about you, Sadie?" Emma asked. "Does this sound like somethin' you'd enjoy?"

All eyes settled on her, and she paused for only a moment. "Yes, I would love to participate."

Everyone started clapping, and Sadie suddenly wondered if they hadn't conspired to make her a mission project, of sorts. For months, she'd harbored a bitter root, daily watering it with her sullenness and utter lack of joy, never mind her lack of any Christmas cheer. Surely, the entire town viewed her as a grouch who'd lost her smile.

Later, crossing the street after everyone had exchanged good-byes, Sadie stopped in front of the Christmas tree to admire it. Something at her feet caught her eye, and she bent to study it in the moonlight. It was a crocheted angel that must have fallen from a branch. She picked it up, then stood there fingering the soft yarn and admiring the handiwork. Someone had poured a great deal of time, effort, and love into creating this small cherub, only for it to wind up on the ground, smudged and soiled. She brushed it off as best she could, then opened the yarn loop at the top of its halo and hung it on the tree, pushing it well back on a sturdy branch to prevent it from falling.

You are My handiwork—My cherished creation. The beautiful words washed over her in a gentle, beckoning manner, and she wondered what had prompted them. Had God planted them in her heart? Surely, she wouldn't have said them of her own accord, for she didn't view herself as anyone special—certainly not of late. She glanced at the angel ornament, then looked skyward. A cluster of clouds passed over the moon, and she marveled that the God who had fashioned so fine a universe could actually consider her His cherished creation.

"Oh, heavenly Father, I sense Your presence," she whispered into the night. She cast one last glance at the festive tree, exhaled a long, contented sigh, and then strode to her apartment, awash with a sense of bottomless peace. The thought occurred to her that, once upstairs, she would brew a cup of tea, then curl up in a chair with her Bible and begin reading through the Psalms. Yes, that was exactly what she would do.

Chapter Nine

Tuesday kept Reed running from morning till night. He knew from the moment he woke up that it was going to be one of those days. First, he'd overslept, something he rarely did, but he'd had such trouble getting to sleep that after he'd finally dozed off, his body had decided to stay asleep right past sunrise.

He blamed Sadie Bennett for his sleepless night. Even though he hadn't seen her since Sunday, he couldn't get her out of his head. He'd spent a good deal of the night in Bible study and in prayer, asking God to heal her from the inside out and give her renewed joy and purpose; and again, he'd sensed a quiet yet clear voice speaking into his spirit that he needed to give her time and also space. In other words, he should stop pursuing her—for the time being, anyway. Yes, she'd loosened up on Sunday, but he wondered how long it would be before she closed up tighter than a drum again. Perhaps in another week he'd peek in on her at Grace's Tearoom to see how she received him. If it were with a cool aloofness, he'd take another step back. Oh, he wasn't about to give up—unless she outright told him she found him about as desirable as a skinned rooster.

He and his assistant, Bart Murphy, worked all morning feeding and watering the horses, mucking out their stalls, and exercising them in the stable out back. He provided full livery for several clients who lived in town but had no space for keeping horses, and he also boarded horses on a short-term basis, whether for an overnight stay or daily during the week while their owners worked in town. He also kept a number of horses and vehicles for rent. Occasionally, folks living in town who didn't have their own means of transportation would rent a horse and rig for a day if they needed to travel a distance. Today was one of those days when customers came and went almost constantly.

Once in a while, an old fellow with nothing better to do would stop in and wait for one of his cronies to come along. For that reason, Reed had fashioned a couple of long benches and stationed them outside at the front of the livery so the menfolk could sit and jabber for hours. The sun shone as bright as a new daisy today, and those benches beckoned a number of old acquaintances. At one point, Reed stepped outside and joked that he might start charging rent for the space they took up. John Holden, former postmaster of Little Hickman, remarked that if he was going to do that, then he ought to provide refreshments, too. Reed laughed and walked back inside.

The first lull in the day didn't come until late afternoon. Reed decided to take advantage of the opportunity to go to the bank. He unlocked and opened the top drawer of the dusty, battered desk at the front of the barn and snatched up his leather moneybag containing the day's transactions. On his way out, he told Bart where he was headed.

"Fine by me," Bart answered. "Just gettin' ready to take old Chester out to the stable for a little exercise." Chester was their oldest horse, a gentle nag who moved slowly and worked out perfectly for youthful riders.

Reed was waylaid by a couple of people on his way to the bank. Irwin Waggoner stopped him first to ask how he liked his new house. They talked a few minutes, Reed telling him about the few repairs and improvements he'd made since moving in—repainting some walls, putting new wallpaper in the living room, and replacing several windows. "I'm just waiting on a few furniture pieces I ordered from Sears, Roebuck & Co. about a month ago, and then I think I'll be done for a while."

"Until you get a wife, anyway," Irwin joshed. "She'll have you changing the wallpaper and paint colors again, to suit her tastes."

The mention of a wife made Reed's heart jump. "Well, I doubt that'll happen anytime soon."

"No? I thought I'd seen you on a few occasions with that pretty, young widow woman who works at Grace's Tearoom."

"You mean Sadie Bennett?" Now his pulse was racing. "I did take her out a couple of times, but there are no wedding plans in the making, believe me."

"Ah, well. Give her time." Waggoner scratched his whiskered jaw and winked. "These things don't happen overnight."

He couldn't imagine what had prompted the man to say that, but he'd be pickled if that wasn't the same message that had been impressed upon his heart the evening before—and on two occasions before that. Did God intend Waggoner's words as another affirmation? In the course of his Bible reading last night, he'd run across a verse in the Twenty-seventh Psalm that said something like, "Wait on the Lord and be of good courage, and He will strengthen your heart. Wait, I say, on the Lord." The words had greatly consoled him as he'd sought God's discernment. If His plan was for Reed and Sadie to be together, then that plan would come to fruition in *God's* time, not his.

After bidding Irwin good-bye, Reed ran into Grace Giles, also on her way to the bank. Grace had moved to Little Hickman a couple of years ago and built a fine business for herself. She'd always struck him as smart and clever, as well as full of godly wisdom.

"You haven't popped in for lunch lately," she said as they fell into step with each other. "Where've you been?"

"Oh, I've been bringing my lunch to work with me," Reed replied. "The livery's been getting too busy for me to leave."

"I see. Hm, and here I thought your absence might have something to do with one of my employees...a lovely young woman named Sadie."

He gave a slight chuckle. "That might play into my reasons. She doesn't seem to want much to do with me. I've decided it's best to take a few steps back for now."

"I see."

"She's as much as admitted she's still in love with her late husband. She said she still thinks about him every day. I'm not prepared to compete with him."

Grace touched his arm, and they stopped on the sidewalk in front of the bank, the town Christmas tree in full view, its branches glistening in the sunlight. A few folks stood at the base, gazing up in admiration, while two boys played a game of chase around it.

"You mustn't let her words deter you," Grace told him. "She's putting up her defenses to prevent herself from further hurt. My husband passed several years ago, and my heart ached with emptiness for months afterward. I think that, had God chosen to bring another man into my life, I, too, might have shied away at first, but I also think I would have recovered much sooner. Oh, don't get me wrong—one never fully recovers from the loss of a spouse. But the day will come when it won't hurt as much to call up the memories. And new love helps to speed the recovery process.

"I don't mean to diminish Sadie's grief, but I do think it's beyond time for her to take her eyes off her sadness and move forward. In my heart of hearts"—she put a gloved fist to her chest—"I believe she's taking giant steps to do that. I've seen subtle changes in her, especially of late."

"Really?"

Grace smiled. "She hummed off and on all day yesterday. She mentioned having had a delightful time the night before with a group of ladies who volunteered to stitch a slew of costumes for the children's Christmas program. And then she spoke about some new ministry, a monthly sewing bee, that Emma Atkins wants to start up after Christmas. I believe she's coming out of that dark place she's been hiding in for so long."

Cautious optimism flowed through Reed. "This is exactly what I've been praying for her."

"As have I, along with who knows how many others about town. What I want to tell you, Reed, is not to give up on her. Just give her time to renew her faith in Christ and discover the hope that is hers through trusting Him."

Give her time. There it was again, that familiar phrase.

"I will, and I am."

She patted his arm in much the same way his mother might do. "Good, that's good. And don't make yourself so scarce at the tearoom."

"I'll be back, don't worry."

The Christmas program rehearsals on Tuesday and Thursday night had not only gone well, they'd proved fun. The children had clearly been practicing their lines at home, and most of them did well when standing on the small platform, although some needed prompting when they forgot a word or two. The youngest ones appeared shy and in need of encouragement, so Sadie knelt down in front of the platform, program in hand, to help urge them on. The little choir sang their hearts out, accompanied by Bess Barrington at the piano, and Nora did a remarkable job with her solo, managing to bring Sadie to tears with her flawless tone and faint vibrato. Sadie had never really heard her sister sing by herself—hadn't even known she had the ability to perform—but when she considered that her mother always sang to her and her siblings at bedtime, it didn't seem so surprising.

Even Jacob Michael amazed her with his knack for standing still for most of the ten-minute stable scene, with the angels making an appearance, followed by the shepherds and finally the three kings. Each child had only a couple of lines, and, fortunately, all that Jacob Michael had to do was stand there and welcome the visitors with an outstretched arm. At one point, he bent down to tie his bootlaces, and then later he leaned over to whisper something to Edward Swain, one of the shepherds, and they started giggling—until Liza Broughton put a stop to their silliness. Having taught school before marrying Ben, she had a fine way of handling the children, using a voice that was firm yet kind.

At the close of the Thursday rehearsal, Emma reminded the children that this had been their final practice before the Christmas Eve program. She gave them each a piece of paper to take home, a letter for the parents, with instructions as to the time they should arrive at the church the following Tuesday night. They would need to arrive in plenty of time for donning their costumes and preparing their minds for the performance.

"Miss Liza, Miss Sadie, and I all want you at the church no later than six o'clock," she told the children. "Be sure to invite your friends and neighbors to come, especially those who may not have a place to go on Christmas Eve. We want everyone to hear the wondrous story of Jesus' birth. In the meantime, it is up to you to keep practicing your pieces with loud, clear voices." She surveyed the group of wide-eyed children. "Y'all did a fine job t'night, and we're so proud of you."

Liza started clapping for them, so Sadie and Emma joined in, as did several parents who'd been sitting at the back of the church.

Sadie turned to gaze out over the small audience, and that's when she spotted him—Reed—standing in the doorway, smiling, with his muscular arms crossed over his broad chest. She wondered how much of the practice he'd watched. Had he been back there the whole time? Not only that, but who was he smiling at? He waved, so she waved back, and when he started moving in her direction, her heart took a surprising leap—until she discovered he hadn't been looking at her at all but at Sarah and Rocky Callahan, who'd come to watch their children prac- tice. He walked up to the bench where they were seated and sat down. She quickly turned herself back around as she felt a foolish twinge of disappointment. Hadn't she declared to Reed that they had nothing in common and told him, in essence, to stop asking her out? She'd pushed him away, even though he'd assured her they could take things slow, and now she thought she had the right to nurse an ache in her gut? Gracious, but she was as fickle as a feather in the wind! She hadn't seen Reed since Sunday, and it occurred to her that she'd been missing him; she just hadn't wanted to admit it till now.

"Thanks for your help tonight, Sadie," Liza said, her voice yanking Sadie out of her musings. "Emma and I surely did appreciate it."

Sadie spun around. "Oh! You're very welcome. Thanks for asking me. I'll be here good and early on Tuesday night. I really can't believe Christmas is coming so fast."

"Nor can I. We put up our Christmas tree a week ago, but we haven't finished our shopping yet."

"Shopping? Shopping!" It struck Sadie that she still had to buy a gift for each of her siblings and something for her father and Miranda. "I'll have to go out tomorrow after work." Until the past few days, she'd had no interest in Christmas, but something had changed in her over the course of the week, and the prospect of finding just the right thing for them filled her with a certain sense of joy and excitement.

"How'd I do on my solo?" asked Nora, coming up beside her.

Sadie wrapped her arms around her sister. "You were wonderful! I had no idea you could sing like that."

"What about me?" asked Jacob Michael. "Was I a good Joseph?"

She ruffled his thick black hair. "You sure did. Just make sure you don't bend down to tie your shoes on the night of the program. I don't think the real Joseph wore lace-up boots."

Little Elizabeth cozied up next to Sadie, wrapping her arms around her waist. "I messed up my piece."

"No, you didn't, honey. I had to help you with only one line." She bent down so that the tips of their noses nearly touched. "And I'll be here Tuesday night to do the same."

"You missed decorating the family tree on Monday night," Daniel said, turning the tide of the conversation with his surprise approach. "Miranda made lots o' goodies, and we had hot cocoa and mulled cider."

Sadie straightened. "Sounds delightful. Papa invited me, but I had already promised to help sew the costumes for the Christmas program. How did the tree turn out?"

"It looks pretty," Nora said. "Papa found a good one right on our property. You'll see it Sunday."

"Is Mr. Reed comin' back to ar house for dinner?" Elizabeth asked Sadie.

"Oh, I hope he does," Nora gushed. "We can tell more funny stories."

"Oh, I...I wouldn't suppose." Sadie involuntarily turned her gaze to the bench Reed had been sharing with the Callahan family. When she saw that it was vacant, she wanted to kick herself for the inexplicable feeling of sullenness that came over her. *Ridiculous*, she inwardly chided herself. Why should she care that he'd left without saying hello?

"He came to hear me sing my solo," Nora announced.

"What?" Sadie frowned. "How do you know that?"

"'Cause Papa an' I saw him in town this afternoon, and I told him I was goin' to practice my song tonight. He promised to come watch. He kept his promise, too, an' smiled at me the whole time I sang, which helped me stay calm. I hope he comes Tuesday night so I can keep my eyes on him again."

"That was...mighty nice of him." Sadie knew she ought to be happy that he'd come, even if had been to see Nora and not her.

"You kids ready to leave?" Daniel asked. "Papa sent me over in the rig to fetch you. We all got school tomorrow." He turned to Sadie. "You want a ride?"

"A ride? Good heavens, no. It's just a short walk."

"Okay, then."

They said their good-byes, and when Emma and Liza assured her that they would handle things from there, she put on her coat and walked back to her quiet little apartment. Alone.

Chapter Ten

The Sunday before Christmas, Little Hickman Community Church had record attendance, making Reed wonder if the parishioners had built a big enough facility. He attributed the large crowd to Jon's preaching and to the invitation he'd extended at the community tree-decorating ceremony. Of course, it being the Sunday before Christmas played a significant role, as most folks, even if they didn't attend church on a regular basis, made it a point to show up for Christmas and Easter.

After squeezing in at the end of the eighth row, Reed fastened his eyes on Sadie, seated three rows ahead of him. She'd stationed herself smack-dab in the middle of her family, with Elizabeth on her lap. The whole group looked dressed to the hilt, the girls in their Sunday hats, and Paul wearing a fine tailored suit, his gray hair slicked back.

Reed, too, had taken a little extra care to spiff up for the service. It was Christmas, after all, and one never could tell what the day might bring. He hoped for a chance to at least say hello to Sadie and see if it led anywhere. It'd been a solid week since he'd last talked with her, and it had taken every morsel of self-control he could muster not to walk into Grace's Tearoom, catch her by the arm when she passed his table, and say, "Look, I'm falling in love with you, and it doesn't seem fair I should keep that a secret." Or some such thing.

More realistically, his words would probably amount to something like, "How have you been? You look lovely, as usual. What's the soup of the day?" He was such a coward, always worried he would say the wrong thing and ruin his chances with her altogether. For that reason, he hadn't even hung around the church after the rehearsal on Thursday night. He'd gotten a glimpse of her helping the children, and that had sufficed for the time being. Better to try to leave her wishing to see more of him than to make an utter pest of himself.

The song leader led the congregation in several Christmas hymns, and Jon delivered a fine message that brought Christmas into its proper perspective—eyes off oneself and on Christ and others, with the primary focus of giving, not receiving. He then invited his wife, Emma, to come forward and explain a new ministry called Creative Kindness Sewing Bee. The ladies of the church were invited to meet once a month at Emma's Boardinghouse to help stitch garments, hats, mittens, scarves, slippers, toys, quilts, afghans, and other items for those less fortunate. "We've formed a committee to get this ministry off the ground," she announced, "and it consists of Iris Winthrop, Bess Barrington, Fancy Jenkins, Sadie Bennett, and myself. We hope t' gather as much interest as we can in this project, and I'd encourage all of you t' give monetarily so that we can purchase fabric and other essential items to get started."

After a few additional words, she sat down, and Jon announced the taking up of a special Christmas offering, the proceeds of which would benefit the new ministry. All around, Reed witnessed fellow parishioners, even those he would have considered less fortunate, dig deep into their pockets. Reed joined them, and as he did, he marveled at the notion of Sadie Bennett serving on the committee. For that reason, he cleaned himself dry of every last penny he could find.

At the conclusion of the service, just before giving the benediction, the reverend encouraged everyone to attend the Christmas Eve service at 7:00 on Tuesday night. Then he dismissed everyone, and folks started making their way toward the door, with plenty of friendly chatter, handshakes, and sounds of excited children finally releasing their bottled-up energy. Reed had full intentions of greeting Sadie, until the elderly Clarence and Mary Sterling hurried over to him. "Say there, young man, you didn't forget you're coming over for Sunday dinner, did you?" Clarence asked, clutching him by the forearm.

Actually, he *had* forgotten. Now he recalled that Mary Sterling had invited him a good month ago, insisting he join them for dinner on the Sunday before Christmas, along with Jon and Emma Atkins. "Are you kidding?" he said. "I wouldn't miss it."

"Well, that's good. The wife, here, has prepared a regular feast. You won't go away hungry."

Reed smiled. "I look forward to sitting at your table."

"We look forward to havin' you," Clarence said. "You come on out t' the farm in half an hour or so. We'll get a head start on y'."

"I'll see you then."

Clarence nudged his wife into the aisle, and they disappeared in a flurry of children bedecked in reds and greens, women wearing fancy hats and festive scarves, and men looking none too shabby in their Sunday best.

After the brief tête-à-tête, Reed scanned the crowd for Sadie, but she'd vanished. Where had she gone in such a hurry? He spotted her father, Daniel, and Jacob Michael moving down the center aisle, so he stepped into the side aisle and made his way to the main entry area. There he saw Miranda, Nora, and Elizabeth speaking with a young family, but nowhere did he see any sign of Sadie.

He kept moving, thinking perhaps he would discover her in the foyer.

"Mr. Harris! Mr. Harris!"

He recognized Nora Swanson's voice before turning.

"You're invited out to ar house again—if you want to come, that is."

"Oh! But...I...." He gave another quick glance around.

"If you're lookin' for Sadie, she shot out ahead of us," the girl explained. "She's makin' the dinner today. When Papa tol' her he was goin' to invite you, she got a little purplish around the neck, but she didn't tell him not to."

"Really?"

"Say, Reed." Paul Swanson appeared at his side, Daniel with him. "Looks like Nora beat me to the invitation. Can you make it today?"

"I—well, I'd like to, but...."

"Sadie's countin' on it," said Daniel. "I mean, she didn't say it in so many words, but she got that shy kind o' look in her eye when Papa told her you'd be comin'."

"I didn't tell her you were coming," Paul assured Reed, then turned to Daniel. "Good grief, don't put words in my mouth, Son." Then he looked back at Reed. "I told her I planned to invite you, that's all."

"I see." Reed's gut twisted into a tight ball of regret. "Well, I'm afraid I can't make it."

"Oh," said Daniel, his face going from cheerful to crestfallen.

"I'm really sorry, but I'd already accepted another invitation to dinner. A particular lady invited me a good month or more ago. I understand the reverend and his wife are also joining us."

Elizabeth rushed over to where they were standing. "Are you comin' over t'day, Mr. Reed?"

"He can't," Daniel announced, still wearing that hangdog face.

"Sugar foot. Well, y'r comin' Christmas Eve to watch me sing, ain't y'?" she asked.

He reached up and touched the tip of her cute nose. "That, my dear, I wouldn't dream of missing."

Sadie took her time on the ride back to town late that afternoon. She'd been struck with the gloomies, and it bothered her immensely. She'd told Reed she wasn't ready for courtship, so why did she feel so dejected? She'd been disappointed to learn that he'd turned down her father's invitation to dinner, but when Daniel had gone on to tell her that he'd accepted an invitation from another lady, and that the reverend and Emma would be joining them, well, it had shot a hole straight through her. Not only had he chosen to stop pursuing her, he'd already started seeing someone else! No wonder he'd stayed away from Grace's Tearoom this entire week. No wonder he hadn't greeted her at the Christmas program rehearsal. And no wonder he hadn't sought her out after church that morning, no matter that she'd made a beeline for home at the close of the service. Why, when she's passed him in the center aisle, he hadn't so much as raised his head to glance at her, so involved had he been in conversing with that elderly couple, the Sterlings.

"Lord, forgive me for my sour attitude," she prayed into the cold wind. Charlie nickered in return. She leaned forward and rubbed his neck, her body moving in natural rhythm with his every stride. "I'm a silly-dilly, Lord, not wanting Reed's attention one minute but craving it the next. What's wrong with me? Oh God, give me a discerning spirit, clearheadedness, and a decisive mind." She made a growling sound that came from deep down. "Right now, I'm such a dunderhead!"

She considered the conversation she'd had with her father that afternoon when he'd stepped into the small library and discovered her browsing the selection of books. "You've been extra quiet today," he'd said. "Something on your mind?"

She'd turned and studied his kind face—the wrinkles around his blue eyes—his gray hair neatly combed and parted in the middle, and his strong build, earned from years of laboring in the fields. "How were you able to marry again so soon after Mama died?"

"Does it bother you that I did?"

"No, not at all. I like Miranda a lot. She's perfect for you. I just don't know how you did it."

If the unexpected topic had fazed him, he hadn't let it show; he'd just massaged his goatee and fixed his eyes on something over her left shoulder as he pondered. "Well, I certainly didn't plan to fall in love again. Quite frankly, it was the last thing on my mind. But when I first laid eyes on Miranda, about five months after your mother's passing, something in me just stirred—came to life, if you will. I knew that after meeting her at that church function in Nicholasville, I had to see her again. There just wasn't any question. From there, our friendship blossomed into love." He'd let his eyes drop to her face, then he'd taken a few steps closer. "When love hits"—he'd balled his hand into a fist and brought it to his chest—"and you feel in your heart that God has

His hand in it, then you go with your gut, and that's what I did with Miranda."

She'd given a couple of slow nods. "I haven't thought about Tom nearly so much these past few weeks. I've started feeling whole again, Papa, but then I feel guilty for it."

"You mustn't. Tom would want you to be happy. Do you ever see yourself falling in love again?"

She'd never had this sort of discussion with her father. "Awkward" wasn't exactly the correct term to describe it. Her father was a loving, gentle, and understanding man. Perhaps "slightly self-conscious" best defined her emotions. "At some point, I suppose."

"With someone I know whose name begins with the letter *R*?"

She'd tilted her head to one side. "Oh, Papa, I've never been good at fooling you."

He'd laughed and placed his hands on her shoulders. "From what I know of him, he's a good man, this Reed Harris."

"But he's with another woman today. Daniel even said."

"Daniel loves to spout at the mouth."

"But...I don't know what to think."

"I know you went on some outings with him a few months ago. Has he continued pursuing you?"

"Yes, but I've declined his advances. I didn't feel ready."

He'd tipped her chin up with his finger. "And now?"

"Now? I...I think I'm ready, but I haven't talked to him even once since last Sunday."

Her father's brow had wrinkled. "I guess there's only one thing you can do, then."

She'd taken a deep breath. "What's that?"

His mouth had quirked with amusement. "Tell him how you feel."

She entered Little Hickman from the east end, so that Reed's Livery was the first business that came into view. She noticed some movement inside and saw a flicker of light through a side window. Out back, a few horses moseyed in the enclosed yard, nibbling at bits of dead grass. It wasn't even four o'clock, but the utter lack of sunshine made the hour seem later. On impulse, she reined in Charlie and stopped in the middle of the street, pondering whether to hitch him to the post and go inside. She'd never had cause to visit the livery before, seeing that Mr. Bordon generously provided her a fine horse and a place to keep him.

"Tell him how you feel." Her father's words echoed almost like a thunderclap, her heartbeat competing with them.

"Oh, Lord, please stop me if I'm not supposed to do this," she prayed. Of course, she heard nothing in reply. "All right, then make him not be here."

She had no idea if her prayer had even reached heaven. Both pleas seemed more like demands—until she recalled a verse from Psalm 138: *"The Lord will perfect that which concerneth me: thy mercy, O Lord, endureth for ever: forsake not the works of thine own hands."* She had to believe, then, that anything troubling or worrisome to her also concerned God; therefore, if she longed to accomplish His will, He would give her the proper words to speak to Reed if he happened to be inside. And if Reed wasn't here, then she would take that to mean that the timing wasn't right for talking to him. She hoped her logic made sense, anyway.

With a measure of reluctance, she directed Charlie to the hitching post, gathered every bit of strength and courage she could manage, and then dismounted, looping the reins over the post. With gloved hands at her sides, she stood and stared at the wooden structure identified by a placard that read "Reed's Livery." She drew in a huge breath, held it, and then released it slowly. "Lord, give me courage," she murmured on her way to the door.

Chapter Eleven

Under normal circumstances, the livery was closed for business on Sundays, with Bart coming in only to feed and water the horses and muck out stalls; but because Christmas was only two days away, and incoming visitors needed provision for their animals, they'd left the "Open" sign in the window. Bart had worked the morning shift, and Reed had come in at three. He would lock up the doors at seven, though, so anyone coming into town after that would have to make do on his own. As it was, Reed had only one empty stall left, and once that was filled, he would post the sign that said "No Availability."

He was cleaning out the empty stall when the front door opened with a creak. "You're in luck," he called to the shadowy figure at the front of the livery. "Got one stall left. Name?"

He got nothing in return, but he could have sworn he'd heard the door and even seen someone—or something. He propped the shovel against the stall gate and wiped his soiled hands on his pant legs, thinking how he couldn't wait to get back to his house for a good hot bath. The negative aspect of working in a livery was the stench that accompanied the job. Usually, when he made his way home, he tried to walk fast with his head down, to minimize his chances of meeting up with anyone who might want to shoot the breeze with him. "Anybody there?" Still no response.

He left the stall and made his way toward the front of the barn. What he saw made his heart clatter in his ears and his feet stop dead in their tracks. He squinted, then blinked twice, to see if the image before him might disappear. "Sadie?" Since she stood with the light silhouetting her, it made identifying her difficult, but he was fairly certain it was Sadie.

"Hello, Reed."

He took in a huff of air. "Well, I'll be dipped in sauce! What brings you here?" Suddenly he got a whiff of his own body odor and nearly drowned in a pool of embarrassment. Yes, he'd been with her immediately after work the night of the tree-decorating ceremony, but at least he'd had a chance to wash the worst of the grime from his hands, face, and arms at the outdoor pump before mingling with the public. Today, he stunk like a skunk. Should he step any closer to her? He doubted it. He scratched his head and, in so doing, pulled several pieces of straw from his hair. *Good grief.* "Um, excuse my...." He looked down at himself, then snatched a damp towel from the side of the washbasin and started wiping his hands vigorously.

She waved a hand. "No matter. I know you're busy. I...I don't even know why I stopped, actually. I...I'll just be going." She turned to leave.

"No, wait!" He stepped forward and snagged her by the arm, then quickly let go so he wouldn't offend her. "I mean, there must be some reason you stopped."

She shrugged, and in the dim light of dusk, he saw her bite her plumpish lower lip as if pondering what to say. "I'm a little...I don't know."

"What?" he urged her, his heart pounding through his coat. The barn was cold, and he worried that her visible shivering would cause her to leave without an explanation. He ventured one step closer. "You're a little what? Nervous?" He didn't want to put words in her mouth, but she needed help.

"Maybe. I've never done this before."

"What? Walked into a smelly barn?" A horse in the back whinnied, as if to make its disapproval known. Reed delivered Sadie a smile that he knew came off crooked. People had always remarked that one side of his mouth often went higher than the other when he grinned.

"No, silly." She clasped her hands in front of her and swiveled her body back and forth in a shy manner, chewing her lip the harder. "I've never called on a man before."

"Oh, I see. Is that what you're doing—calling on me? I'm flattered if you are." He felt his shoulders drop as he began to relax.

"You—I—*we* haven't talked for an entire week."

"I know. That was intentional."

Her mouth opened, but a long pause followed. "I see," she finally said. "Well, that settles that, then." She started to turn once more, but he snagged hold of her again, not letting go this time.

"What do you mean? What's settled?"

She looked down at her pointy-toed boots peeking out from beneath her navy blue skirt, and her hat brim covered most of her face.

He gently lifted her chin with a curled forefinger. "Nothing's settled, Sadie Bennett. When I said it was intentional, I meant I kept my distance because I didn't want to press you into anything you weren't prepared to start. I thought you'd want it that way."

She brushed his hand away, whether due to the stench or his touch, he couldn't say. "Well, it surely didn't take you long to start up with someone else, now, did it?"

"What?"

"I am not going to start up anything with anyone, Reed Harris, especially not with someone as fickle as the weather."

"What are you talking about?" Now she'd gotten *his* dander up. "I'm about as fickle as a grizzly bear. When I told you I wanted to court you, I meant it. Every word."

"Then why did you dine at the home of another lady today?" She asked the question with a bit of sass in her voice, her body tipped slightly forward. "And don't deny it, because Daniel reported what you announced to him and Papa at church this morning."

Reed put three fingers to his mouth to cover his grin. "I announced it, did I?" he said behind his hand.

"And stop laughing at me. You must take me for a fool."

"Sadie Bennett, if I didn't stink to high heaven, I'd kiss you right now."

She gasped. "You most certainly would not."

"Would, too. You're jealous, and do you know how happy that makes me?"

"I am not jealous, you—you—you arrogant so-and-so."

In two seconds flat, she spun on her boot heel and, with skirt flaring, made a beeline for the door. He set off after her, snatching her coat sleeve just before she stepped outside. "Just hold it right there, young lady." This time, he didn't worry about his stinking self. She refused to face him, so he applied enough pressure to turn her around. She acquiesced but kept her gaze lowered. The stubborn little *so-and-so!* May as well give her the same name. He'd never imagined she had this side to her, but he rather liked it.

"First of all," he started in a quiet voice, "I did have dinner with a lady today—a lady *and* her husband. Furthermore, they are old enough to be my grandparents. You know Clarence and Mary Sterling, don't you? They invited me to dinner about a month ago, and I accepted."

Her head raised ever so slowly, and their eyes met. Clearly, the reality of the truth had dawned. Her mouth formed an *o*.

He bent at the waist to get a better assessment of her dark, mesmerizing eyes. "Are you satisfied?"

She pursed her lips and gave three fast nods. "What I really am is embarrassed."

"Don't be." He gave a slight pause. "Sadie...." He wanted to put his thoughts in proper order so they'd come out right when he voiced them. He loosened his hold on her arm and set to caressing it. She didn't try to step away, which gave him great hope. "Were you seriously concerned I might have eyes for someone else?"

Rather than answer, she started to tear up, and he melted into a mound of mush.

"It's okay to feel again, Sadie. Tom would want it. I never met him, but I have to believe he was a good man to have won your heart. And because of that—because he must have been a man of great integrity and wisdom—I know in my heart that he would want you to live your life to the fullest, with someone who would love you as much as, or maybe even more than, he ever could. I realize your time with him was short. Don't you want to start afresh?"

She sniffed, swiping at her damp cheeks with her coat sleeve. "But, what if...what if something happens?"

"What do you mean?"

She gave another loud sniff, her eyes filling to the point that her tears dripped down her cheeks like two little rivers. "What if I give my heart to somebody else"—her voice trembled and shook—"and the Lord decides to take him, too? Then what?"

He didn't care about protocol or manners, or even that he smelled clear to the next county. He removed her hat and tossed it to the side, caring not where it landed, and wrapped her in a strong embrace, his arms reaching fully around her, pulling her tight against his chest, then rocked her gently back and forth, back and forth. Slowly, her arms went around his back, and he felt her hands lock together. "Sadie, honey. Sweet lady," he whispered against her hair, then rested his chin on her head. For a full minute or more, he said nothing, just rocked and held while she let her emotions flow. How long had it been since she'd allowed herself to cry with abandon in front of another living soul? *Lord, she needs to know the depth of Your love—that, no matter what the future holds, she always has You.*

In due time, her sobs slowed to hiccupping sighs, and though he didn't want to, he set her back from him and gazed down into her swollen eyes, now ravaged with dark red circles. He loved her—that much he knew from the depths of his soul and beyond. He didn't have to know everything about her to be certain that his love would only grow stronger the more he learned about her. He dried her cheeks with the pads of his thumbs. "There are no guarantees in life, Sadie, only that God promises to walk with us through every circumstance. Can you trust Him enough to not give in to your fears for the future? If you make Him the Lord of your life, then He will be your first love, which is how it should be. Putting Him in that rightful spot in your heart removes fear and leaves in its place a deep sense of peace and joy."

She blinked a few times and tilted her head to the side while looking up at him. "You are such a brilliant man, Reed Harris. I think I like you—quite a lot, in fact."

"Do you, Sadie Bennett? Because I like you a lot, as well."

They exchanged smiles until her face grew serious. "I want to rid myself of fear, Reed, and I know the only way I can do that is to grow in my faith. I'm working on that."

"It's enough that you're working at it. God will honor you for it and will help you on your journey. You'll see. Plenty of people have been praying for you."

She nodded. "I've felt their prayers."

A moment of silence passed between them as they simply exchanged looks.

Finally Reed sniffed the air and wrinkled his nose. "I stink to high heaven, don't I?"

She laughed. In fact, she couldn't stop, and she had to put a hand to her stomach. "I wasn't going to say it," she said when she'd regained some of her composure.

"Oh, blast. It goes with the job."

"I know, but it's okay. I don't mind. I grew up on a farm, remember?"

Her laughter died, and they both sobered. Reed stared at her for all of ten heartbeats. There was no sound but the uneven breaths coming between them.

"May I...?" he murmured. "Could I...?"

"Yes," she answered, "you may." And she lifted her face to make it easier for his lips to find hers in a first kiss, one that would mark the beginning of something special and sweet and even God-ordained. Apparently, she didn't mind his barn smell, for she tightened her grasp around him, spreading her palms wide across his shoulder blades. The kiss went on for some time before they both realized their need for air. They pulled apart, breathed deeply, and drank in the other's face before moving in for one more taste of each other.

At the rear of the livery, two horses neighed back and forth, and in the distance, a group of carolers lifted their voices in song. "Joy to the world! The Lord is come; let earth receive her King."

Chapter Twelve

Sadie, I'm scared," Nora confessed just minutes before the Christmas program was to begin. If Little Hickman Community Church had met its maximum seating last Sunday, tonight it was bursting at the seams, with menfolk standing at the back and in the aisles and everybody else squeezed together on the wooden benches like toes trying to fit in a shoe two sizes too small. Excitement sizzled as folks chattered none too quietly and babies cried in spurts and sputters.

"Let's say a quick prayer, then," Sadie suggested, taking Nora's hand and pulling her to a spot behind the piano where no one could see them. She put her arm around Nora's shoulders and hugged her close, then whispered a prayer for courage and a healthy dose of self-assurance. "Lord, most of all, we pray that Your name will be honored as Nora sings, that those present who may not know You will be challenged to surrender their hearts and lives to You before they go to sleep tonight." After closing the prayer, she kissed Nora's cheek and gave her one final squeeze. "You'll do fine, honey. You inherited Mama's singing talent and her beauty. Just look at you in that pretty blue dress."

Nora managed a shaky smile and took a big breath. "Thanks. I feel better now."

"Good. Prayer makes all the difference."

Nora gave her a quizzical squint. "You're different, Sadie."

"I am?"

"Yes. Something's happened to you, and I think I know what."

"Do you now?"

"Yup. Reed Harris."

Sadie studied her sister and sighed. "You're very perceptive. Reed is part of it, yes, but it's more than that. I've found my joy again. I've started crawling out of the pit I landed in when Tom died, and I'm discovering that I don't have to live my life wallowing in grief. Reed helped me to realize that, but so did Papa, and you and Jacob Michael and Grace Giles, and…well, a lot of people. Even Iris Winthrop, as grumpy as she can be, played a role. I'm putting Jesus first, and that, my dear sister, is the key. Now, when you sing that song tonight, you be singing it right from your heart, you hear?"

Nora gave a few fast nods, snagged another whopping breath, and pulled her shoulders back. "I'll be keepin' my eyes on Reed, too, 'cause his smile helps me."

Sadie knew just what she meant. The man had a strength about him that worked like a soothing salve to the soul. Her eyes sought him in the crowd and found him looking at her from his spot at the end of the sixth bench from the front, as if he'd heard his name spoken. He'd arrived a full forty-five minutes early to claim his seat, and while she'd scurried about helping children with their costumes, seating them according to the order in which they would perform, and trying to maintain some semblance of calm, she'd felt his smiling gaze on her. Every so often, they'd exchanged a warm glance that had made her want to melt right into the floor. Two rows behind Reed were Grace Giles and, of all people, Sheriff Murdock. The two had started courting just two weeks ago, and they were "moving right along," as Grace had put it. Sadie smiled when she recalled how adamantly Grace had denied any romantic interest in the good sheriff in early December.

Nora sang a flawless solo, her tone rising and falling in just the right places, the words coming out as clear as a bell, and her pitch as perfect as an expertly tuned piano. Jacob Michael behaved himself, for the most part, in his Joseph role, except that he bent down to pick up some straw and throw it at one of the shepherds. Liza's stern face must have had some effect, for he quickly sobered and went back to leaning on his staff and gazing at the baby Jesus. Truly, he had no idea the significance of his role, but it didn't matter; the audience delighted in his carefree, oblivious spirit, snickering at his innocent antics.

Margaret Swain, on the other hand, played the part of Mary with utmost sincerity, every so often casting Jacob Michael a menacing glare when his performance didn't quite measure up to her standards. A few of the children, Elizabeth included, needed a bit of help with their Christmas pieces, but standing on the platform in their impeccable little hand-sewn costumes made up for any missteps. In fact, every child's performance, whether faultless or flawed, seemed to come off as perfect in everyone's eyes, earning the cast hearty applause with only a few giggles. When the children's choir ended the program by singing "O Little Town of Bethlehem," the older ones leading the younger, Sadie found herself having to wipe away yet another round of tears. Gracious, she'd turned into a blubbering fool.

After Reverend Jon offered a closing prayer and then wished everyone a merry Christmas, he announced that Clyde and Iris Winthrop would be standing at the back of the church to hand out small bags of candy to the children. Youthful gasps of delight filled the sanctuary, and the children fairly stampeded toward the doors, the parents doing their best to maintain control.

"Thank you for all your help, Sadie. It was such a pleasure working with you."

Sadie turned at Emma's voice and smiled. "Actually, it was *my* pleasure," she said. "I'm glad you asked me."

Emma leaned forward and whispered, "I see a very good-looking man making his way through the crowd to get to you."

Sadie's stomach rolled over with anticipation, but she forced herself not to turn around. "Does he have brown hair and green eyes?"

"Indeed," Emma said. "And a charming, crooked sort of grin. In fact, he's wearing it now—the grin. Next to my Jon, he's probably the handsomest man in town."

Sadie giggled. "I believe you're right."

Emma put her hand on Sadie's forearm. "There is something quite miraculous about new love—especially when it blossoms at Christmastime."

"No one's said anything about love," Sadie reminded her.

"Yet." Emma winked. "Merry Christmas, honey."

She scooted away before Sadie had a chance to return the sentiment, as two large hands planted themselves on her shoulders and gave a gentle squeeze. She turned her head and looked up into those emerald eyes—eyes that spoke of new beginnings and fresh promises. She couldn't help the smile that broke out on her lips—or the skip of her heartbeat.

"Hi," they said in unison, then chuckled a little.

"I missed you while I was sitting back there"—he hooked a thumb over his shoulder—"and you were up front helping make the program go smoothly. It was worth it, though, because I got to watch you in action."

She giggled, fighting down jumpy nerves. Was this real? Were they a courting couple? *Oh Lord, this feels good. Thank You.* She didn't have to look around to know that people were observing their every move. Strange how it didn't bother her one bit.

They fought their way through the crowd to meet her father, Miranda, and her siblings by the door. They had bundled up and were readying themselves for going out into the brisk air.

Nora spotted them first. "Reed!" she called over a few heads. "I saw you back there smiling at me when I was singing. Thanks for calming my nerves."

"I'm glad to hear it, but I couldn't possibly have listened to you without smiling. You have the voice of an angel."

"Are you comin' over for Christmas Eve?" asked Daniel, directing his gaze at Sadie. "Miranda cooked a big ham."

"Well, of course she is," Papa answered for her. "It wouldn't be Christmas Eve without the whole family together, now, would it? And, Reed, you'll join us."

It wasn't a question. Reed looked at Sadie, and she shot him a hopeful smile.

"Well, sir, it just so happens I'm free tonight."

They all breathed happy sighs.

Elizabeth squealed. "Can I ride with Sadie an'—"

"No," their father said. "We came here as a family, and we will go home as one." He looked over the heads of the younger children and winked at Reed.

"Well then, we'll see you over at the house," Reed said.

"Yes, and bring your appetites," Miranda put in.

Reed had parked his rig in the field next to the church along-side several other buggies. On the walk, he snagged hold of Sadie's hand. It was a perfect fit, her hand in his. A single snowflake landed on her face, followed by another, and then another. She stopped and looked skyward. "It's snowing, Reed." She stretched out a gloved palm. "Isn't it lovely?"

He leaned down and touched his lips to her cheek. "More than lovely."

She shivered. "You said we would go slow, remember?"

He smiled, straightened, and touched the tip of her nose. "I remember. In fact, I'll leave it to you to set the pace. How does that sound?"

She bit down on her lower lip. "It sounds…scary. What if I don't go fast enough to suit you?"

He cradled her cheek with his big, bare hand. "Impossible. Any pace you set is fine by me. I have all the time in the world."

Her heart felt too small to contain her joy. "I didn't buy you a Christmas present. I bought one for everyone else in my family, but I didn't think to get one for you."

"Phew! That's good, because I didn't buy one for you, either."

She heaved a happy sigh. "There's always next year."

He lifted one eyebrow and shot her that crooked grin. "And the year after that?"

"Yes. And then the year after *that*."

They smiled for the length of several happy heartbeats.

"Should we kiss on it?" he asked.

She peeked around the wagon to make sure no one was coming. The coast was clear. "Absolutely."

His hands cupped the sides of her face as tenderly as if he held a bouquet of delicate flowers. She closed her eyes and gave him license, and he touched her mouth with his own. Then he pulled back and looked at her, eyebrows raised, and she gave a tiny shake of her head, knowing innately the question that was on his mind: Was she thinking about Tom when she kissed him?

"I don't think about him nearly as often," she admitted, "and when I do, it's with a love that isn't pained but rather grateful for the love he gave me and also glad that I'm free to move on."

She saw the relief wash over him. He kissed her again, lightly...as lightly as the snow falling around them.

And she thought his name over and over. *Reed...Reed... Reed....*

At long last, the loneliness and pain of her loss had stopped hurting altogether, and the heart once schooled to reject the miracle of newfound love sprouted wings and soared.

Season's Greetings from the Author

Christmas 2014

My dear, loyal readers,

Oh, how I loved revisiting the town of Little Hickman, Kentucky, for this seasonal novella. It's hard to believe that book one in the Little Hickman Creek Series, *Loving Liza Jane*, was published seven years ago—and yet, returning after all this time felt very much like going home to faithful friends and family. Over the years, countless readers have written to me, begging me to continue the series; so when my publisher, Whitaker House, approached me about writing a Christmas story set in my own beloved Little Hickman, Kentucky, I jumped at the opportunity! It was indeed a pleasure to revisit Liza, Sarah, and Emma (and the handsome men in their lives), as well as to introduce you to Little Hickman's newest citizens, Sadie Bennett and Reed Harris.

One question repeatedly asked of me is whether Little Hickman, Kentucky, is a "real" place. Well, I can honestly tell you that it *was* a real place at one time. Situated in Jessamine County, it had its own established post office in the mid-1800s and possibly a general store, too.

Little Hickman Creek still exists to this day, and you can even locate it on a map if you happen to be wearing a good pair of glasses or have a magnifying glass handy. Upon first discovering the little creek years ago using a computer search engine, I innately knew that I would write a series centered on it. One of my daughters and her husband attended Asbury College in Wilmore, Kentucky (in the Lexington region), and my husband and I made countless trips south from Michigan to visit them there. Over the course of that time, I fell in love with Kentucky—its rolling hills; its acres upon acres of farmland; its bluegrass, the richest you will ever see in your lifetime; and its countless miles of white wood fencing containing some of the most beautiful horses in the world.

Whenever I'm working on a novel, I pray over the story and plead with God for guidance and direction, asking Him to implant in my head exactly what He wants the plot to entail and how He wants it to unfold, as well as what He might want to speak into the hearts of my readers through the words I write. It was no different with *Christmas Comes to Little Hickman Creek*. All of my stories are wrought from some sort of pain, sorrow, loss, or deep regret, but as they unfold, the reader begins to see the power of God at work in the midst of each circumstance.

That is not to say that every ending comes off flawless. In case you haven't noticed, life can be messy, and it doesn't always result in happiness for all. What does come, though—if we learn to place our trust fully in Christ—is a sense of His divine plan and presence in the middle of hardship, His healing in heartache, and His purpose in the midst of pain. I always endeavor to make Romans 8:28 come to life for my readers: *"And we know that all things work together for good to them that love God, to them who are the called according to his purpose."*

If you've already read the original three books in the Little Hickman Creek series, then I hope you enjoyed this return trip as much as I have. On the other hand, if this is your first taste of this lovely little community, I hope you've enjoyed your stay. I also hope you'll consider "visiting" one of the towns featured in my other series, if you haven't already: Sandy Shores, Michigan (The Daughters of Jacob Kane); Wabash, Indiana (River of Hope); and Paris, Tennessee (Tennessee Dreams).

You can find my books at ChristianBook.com, Amazon.com, and a host of other online retailers; at Barnes & Noble, Family Christian Stores, and other bookstores; as well as at your local library. Please feel free to visit my Web site at www.sharlenemaclaren.com or to find me on Facebook!

Christmas is a time of joy and laughter for many, while it is bittersweet for others. Whatever the case may be for you, I pray the Lord's endearing presence in your life during this beautiful season of life and love.

Joy and God's richest blessings on each of you,
Sharlene MacLaren

PS: (I just cannot write a letter without a postscript!) In chapter five of *Christmas Comes to Little Hickman Creek*, having just decorated the Christmas tree and sung several carols, the townsfolk gather together at the church for cookies and hot cocoa. I thought it might be fun if I shared with you a Christmas cookie recipe that I've been using for the past forty-five years. In fact, this is the very recipe I used when my daughters were small and we'd decorate a couple dozen cookies of various shapes with multicolored frostings, adding sprinkles and other decorative toppings. Of course, it wouldn't be right if I didn't also include instructions for making the hot cocoa I enjoyed as a child. It was passed down to me from my mother long before hot chocolate packets came into existence! Here are the recipes, along with one last wish for a blessed Christmas!

Roll-and-Cut Christmas Cookies

Approximate yield: Between 2 and 3 dozen cookies (depending on the size(s) of cookie cutters you select)

Ingredients:

4 cups all-purpose flour

2½ teaspoons double-acting baking powder

½ teaspoon salt

⅔ cup shortening

1½ cups granulated sugar

2 eggs

1 teaspoon vanilla extract

4 teaspoons milk

Directions:

1. In a medium bowl, sift together flour, baking powder, and salt. Set aside.
2. In a mixing bowl, cream shortening, sugar, eggs, and vanilla until very light and fluffy. Add flour mixture, alternately with milk, until stiff and well blended.
3. Refrigerate dough until easy to handle, preferably two hours. (You may hasten process by placing the bowl in the freezer for half an hour.)
4. Heat oven to 400 degrees F. On lightly floured surface, roll out one half or one third of the dough at a time, keeping the

rest of the dough in the refrigerator. For crisp cookies, roll dough paper-thin. For softer cookies, roll dough to a quarter of an inch thick.

5. With floured cookie cutter, cut dough into desired shapes. Arrange cookies half an inch apart on lightly greased cookie sheet.

6. Bake 9 minutes, or until very delicately brown. Do not overbake. (Oven temperatures will vary.)

7. Transfer cookies to a baking rack to cool.

8. When the cookies have cooled, decorate according to your preference—with frosting, sprinkles, and so forth. (Hint: Children are very helpful in making this process tons of fun!)

Hot Cocoa for Two

Ingredients:

2 cups whole milk

2 tablespoons unsweetened cocoa powder

4 tablespoons granulated sugar

1 teaspoon vanilla extract

whipped cream, chocolate syrup, and sprinkles to serve (optional)

Directions:

1. In a medium saucepan, combine whole milk, cocoa powder, and sugar.

2. On the stovetop, turn the burner to high and bring mixture to a boil, stirring continuously.

3. Remove from heat and stir in vanilla extract.

4. Divide mixture evenly between two mugs and add a small amount of milk to cool, if desired.

5. To serve, top with a dollop of whipped cream, a drizzle of chocolate syrup, and some sprinkles.

6. Enjoy, preferably in front of a crackling fireplace and a decorated Christmas tree.

About the Author

*B*orn and raised in west Michigan, Sharlene attended Spring Arbor University. Upon graduating with an education degree in 1971, she taught second grade for two years, then accepted an invitation to travel internationally for a year with a singing ensemble. In 1975, she married her childhood sweetheart. Together they raised two lovely, wonderful daughters, both of whom are now happily married and enjoying their own families. Retired in 2003 after thirty-one years of teaching, "Shar" loves to read, sing, travel, and spend time with her family—in particular, her wonderful, adorable grandchildren!

A Christian for forty-five-plus years and a lover of the English language, Shar has always enjoyed dabbling in writing—poetry, fiction, various essays, and freelancing for periodicals and newspapers. Her favorite genre, however, has always been romance. She remembers well writing short stories in high school and watching them circulate from girl to girl during government class. "Psst," someone would whisper from two rows over, when the teacher had his back to the class, "pass me the next page."

In recent years, Shar felt God's call upon her heart to take her writing pleasures a step further and in 2006 signed a contract for her first faith-based novel, launching her writing career with the contemporary romance *Through Every Storm*. With a dozen of her books now gracing store shelves nationwide, she daily gives God all the praise and glory for her accomplishments.

Through Every Storm was Shar's first novel to be published by Whitaker House, and in 2007, the American Christian Fiction Writers (ACFW) named it a finalist for Book of the Year. The acclaimed Little Hickman Creek series consists of *Loving Liza Jane* (Road to Romance Reviewer's Choice Award); *Sarah, My Beloved* (third place, Inspirational Readers' Choice Award 2008); and *Courting Emma* (third place, Inspirational Reader's Choice Award 2009). *Christmas Comes to Little Hickman Creek* is a special add-on to this beloved trilogy. Shar's popular series The Daughters of Jacob Kane comprises *Hannah Grace* (second place, Inspirational Reader's Choice Award 2010), *Maggie Rose*, and *Abbie Ann* (third place, Inspirational Reader's Choice Award 2011). After that came River of Hope, composed of *Livvie's Song*, *Ellie's Haven*, and *Sofia's Secret*. *Threads of Joy* follows *Heart of Mercy* in her latest series, Tennessee Dreams.

Shar has done numerous countrywide book signings, television and radio appearances, and interviews. She loves to speak for women's organizations, libraries, church groups, women's retreats, and banquets. She is involved in Apples of Gold, a mentoring program for young wives and mothers, and is active in her church, as well as two weekly Bible studies. She and her husband, Cecil, live in Spring Lake, Michigan, with their beautiful white collie, Peyton, and their beloved cat, Blue.